Fred Loads

THE BOOK OF
CLASSIC OLD ROSES

Frühlingschnee

THE
BOOK OF
CLASSIC
OLD ROSES

TREVOR GRIFFITHS

Michael Joseph — London

Also by Trevor Griffiths
The Book of Old Roses

First published in Great Britain by
Michael Joseph Limited
27 Wrights Lane, London W8
1987

Griffiths, Trevor, 1928-
    The book of classic old roses.
    1. Roses — New Zealand — Varieties
    I. Title
    635.9'33372   SB411

ISBN 0 7181 2836 2

Designed and produced by Whitcoulls Publishers in New Zealand

Typeset by Whitcoulls Production Ltd, Christchurch
Photo-Litho by Colorite Lithographics Ltd, Auckland
Printed by South China Printing Co, Hong Kong

For my wife Dixie

Arvensis

Célina

CONTENTS

All photographs taken by the author
in his own display garden.

Rambling Rector

FOREWORD

Trevor Griffiths is a rose missionary, spreading the knowledge and love of roses with admirable zest. By the publisher's figures — which I take on trust in preference to counting — the first volume, *The Book of Old Roses*, described almost 600 roses and illustrated over 400 of them. It could, thereby, claim equal rank with a number of worthy books on old roses; but not necessarily pre-eminence.

It was a brilliant idea to extend the work to a second volume, with another 600 varieties and 400 photographs, bringing the total of the two volumes to 1200 roses, of which 800 are illustrated. What a wonderful pool of rose knowledge and reference for rose lovers to drink and browse at! I see no reason why volumes three and four and five should not continue the Griffiths' Rose Encyclopedia.

The roses are 'old' only in character or history. For the author acknowledges that old roses can be born again today. The rose breeder has a facility denied any worker in the animal kingdom, that he can use as parents living things from previous centuries.

In this book, the reader may expect to find a few roses he knows well, such as 'Shot Silk'; a great many names from the past, like 'Château de Clos Vougeot'; and a multitude that had no lodgement in the brain at all, perhaps 'Caporosso' or 'Hugo Roller'. Best of all, the dimly-remembered flicker back on the screen of one's consciousness, aided by simple pictures and a few deft words.

This second volume has the advantage over the first that the more common varieties were already dealt with, and that rarer, often more interesting roses were candidates for inclusion. The author's enthusiasm carries him through his pages; he is like a prospector panning old gold; and believe me, this is a gold mine of a rose book.

JACK HARKNESS
OBE, DHM.

Ruhm von Steinfurth

INTRODUCTION

That I was asked to put together my thoughts, experience and photographs for the first volume, *The Book of Old Roses*, and that they came back to me in the form of a beautiful book was quite unbelievable and exciting. That I have now been asked to assemble a companion volume, so soon after the first, is even more exciting.

There is no repetition of varieties or material between the two volumes and, combined, they describe over 1200 varieties with nearly 800 photos.

The basic format of this volume follows that of the first. All the information is again given in clear, non-technical language with approachable descriptions of the roses. Again I have taken all the photographs here in the display garden at Arowhenua, a fact that is important for two reasons. Firstly, as all the photographs are taken of flowers and plants actually growing in my garden, there is nothing artificial about the arrangement of the flowers, they are taken as is and where is on the plant. The plates therefore show how the roses will appear in your garden. And secondly, the pictures are so natural and untouched that you will find damaged petals, bees and even aphides present — which just goes to show you that in my world of old roses, everything is not perfect.

It is my earnest wish that you will enjoy this book, that you will perhaps learn from it and, more importantly, that you may learn to love the Queen of Flowers as she should be loved.

As a result of the tremendous upsurge in interest all over the world, there are very few roses in this book which are not available in the UK or US. And if some of them are unavailable at the moment, it might make people ask for them and that would be a good thing. An approximation only has been given for heights since these depend on the many soil types, climates and treatments that roses may receive; also, the height of a plant can be very different when the plant is grafted or grown from a cutting.

PART ONE

Salute to
the Rose

A thing of beauty is a joy for ever:
Its loveliness increases; it will never
Pass into nothingness.

Keats

Allen Chandler

Salute to the Rose

When putting pen to paper at the start of this second volume, my thoughts turn to those who, throughout history, have given us so much through their work with and love of roses. It would be my dearest wish that those people could see the fruits of their labours, or know that their efforts were not wasted. One thing is certain—their hard-earned knowledge should not go unheeded. This is perhaps what has motivated me to collect, propagate, display and make available to people in every corner of the world as many old-rose varieties as can be found. It has become apparent through my contacts in other countries that there are many more old varieties surviving worldwide than I had realised. Far from being unknown, they are types which have helped to form the basis of the various families within the genus. That we have been able to track them down, bring them to our nursery in New Zealand and eventually grow them to be seen and cherished is what has inspired me to write this book.

These roses, which spread across all the families, are absolutely beautiful. From the earliest species to the forerunners of the modern roses, they vary in every possible way. Some of them are of such antiquity that no one can accurately tell their age, while others are of comparatively recent origin.

One important result of our endeavours is that like the zoos and game parks around the world, we are preserving these old treasures so that they shall not be lost. By distributing them to rose lovers everywhere, we are making doubly sure that this will not happen. Not only do these old beauties have all the often-mentioned attributes, but many of them have an inner strength that is much sought after by modern hybridists. They have realised that by following the line of breeding used by their own particular establishments for many years, they were perhaps getting colour and precious little else. In their continuing search for something new, hybridists in Europe and, more recently, elsewhere have adopted the policy of using one old rose as either the pollen or seed parent. That the roses will eventually gain strength and health, if nothing else, is quite certain.

From the most recent catalogues received from those rose-growing nurseries that carry out hybridising programmes, it seems certain that there will be many changes in the rose world, mostly attributable to the strong influence of the old roses. No one knows for sure the future direction of rose breeding, but it does seem that many types not at present known or recognised will one day grace the gardens of the world.

I feel that this is an opportune moment to write about the identification of old roses. Because many of the varieties that have survived to the present day originated so long ago, we have only comparatively vague descriptions of those which were known during the Middle Ages, and no descriptions at all of those from earlier times. Yes, ancient writers and artists have left behind their interpretations of those first recorded roses, as have those who came after them—those pioneers of rose culture, devotees who made the time to record their observations, both with their writings and drawings. All have recorded what they have seen, and we the enthusiasts of today must of necessity stand on their shoulders. Nevertheless the accurate naming of some of the old roses will always be a difficult and complex task. Of course, many types have names that are generally agreed upon but there are still many whose titles remain uncertain.

Having heard doubts expressed over the years about the names of quite a number of roses, we too have become suspicious about some of them. Some time ago now, I thought my parent plant of the gallica 'Camaieux' was losing its vigour and duly went through the process of importing another from overseas. I was delighted to see the young plants in quarantine growing well, and looked forward to producing a healthy line of this beautiful rose in the future. But it was not to be, because the freshly imported one was in fact different to mine. It was striped, but in a finer or narrower way, and of course I began to wonder just who has the correct one.

Then again, I am always a little apprehensive about someone who judges two varieties and unequivocally says they are the same. It is a brave person who makes a decision like that. At certain times of the season it is not too hard to find several roses which at the same stages look alike but which, after twelve months, show real differences. No effort is spared in trying to name a plant correctly, and I will again emphasise that to supply a colour photograph or flower is usually not enough. Identification by comparison is the only satisfactory method and even then it may prove unsuccessful. When one considers the many thousands of roses that have come and gone over the last 200 years, for instance, it is remarkable that we can be certain about the name of any particular one. There was a time, for example, when it was commonplace for a nurseryman to grow hundreds of seedlings of *R. spinosissima*, the Scotch or Burnet rose, and probably each one of them was different. It is recorded that one nursery in the United Kingdom listed more than 200 varieties.

Therefore it must have been possible for cottage gardeners and others to grow them from seed, so it is conceivable that there could have been many hundreds of varieties of this rose when it was at the peak of its popularity, although comparatively few of them have been handed down to us to admire today. And can we be sure that those few have been named correctly?

In the late 1600s, *R. gallica* seedlings were raised by the thousand in Europe and many have survived to the present day. Confusion still reigns over the naming of some of them. Some have survived on merit; others perhaps because they had an important name attached to them. Some of the difficulties are caused by the flourishing of roses in certain districts under names that become very well known within that particular area, but elsewhere are not known.

Pierre-Joseph Redouté, the man who painted roses and other plants, has left us a marvellous record of the details of the roses of his time. Redouté was born in Belgium in 1759 and throughout his life he wanted only to paint flowers. He came from a humble family and lived his life doing what he loved most. He rubbed shoulders with the great of his time but never lost the humility he was born with. He perfected a method of drawing and painting roses that has become the standard for work of this kind. The fine detail that he was able to achieve and his accurate reproduction of the colours has made his work much sought after in the identification of the roses of his period. Although we will never have the benefit of seeing the originals, we are fortunate indeed to have access to many fine copies and prints. If you compare one of the excellent copies of Redouté's work with the flowers of the rose in question, you will be surprised at how easy it is to identify your unknown rose.

The only problem which can arise from the use of drawings, paintings and photographs of old roses is that with the passage of time many of the names have been changed. Nevertheless they are still an important means of identification.

It is so disappointing when we discover that an incorrectly named rose has been sent to us in New Zealand, especially after going through all the problems of importation, including taking it through the quarantine process. Each season seems to present us with a different set of difficulties. It is always necessary of course to plant sufficient strong-growing root-stocks to receive the incoming budwood from overseas. They must be grown in a segregated area, and should the expected rose material not arrive, those particular root-stocks are wasted. Some years ago now, a shipment was expected from

West Germany and a letter was duly received advising that it had been sent. Some days went by and it was obvious that there had been a hold-up somewhere along the line. It usually takes about eight days by air mail post from Hamburg. Some six weeks after posting day the parcel arrived. Needless to say, it was too long in transit and the wood was black, mushy and useless.

On another occasion a batch of wood was expected from Europe, but the ideal budding period came and went and there was still no sign of it. A telephone call was put through to the growers in question and we were told that everything was frozen and that the required wood could not be cut. It mattered little that the root-stocks were waiting and that the order had been placed four months previously.

Difficulty can arise at this end too. Recently I wished to send a group of plants to Denmark. They were made ready and a health certificate from the Ministry of Agriculture and Fisheries was applied for. The next day a field officer arrived and told me that the Ministry's regulations simply did not allow for rose exports to Denmark. A timely telephone call proved that the Danish authorities were happy to receive the plants, provided our health certificate complied with their wishes. From all this it must be obvious that we will go to any lengths to share with others these roses which set the nerves tingling with their beautiful form and fragrance.

Roses have been loved and admired throughout the ages and many intriguing tales, be they fact or fancy, have been recorded about the Queen of Flowers.

It has been said that the pruning of roses began during the time of the first King Georges of England. The roses of the day were probably albas, gallicas, damasks and centifolias, and, as was the fashion of the time, no pruning of the plants was carried out at all. It was usual for the palace gardeners, under the guidance of the head gardener, to rake up all the leaves and twigs from the deciduous trees and shrubs about the grounds. These were taken to vacant sites and burned and the resultant ashes suitably distributed. One gardener, who perhaps was lazy or thought he knew more than the others, assembled his heap of leaves and rubbish near one of the rose beds. The fire burned fiercely and, unfortunately for him, there was a wind change. The flames very quickly enveloped the tall rose plants with disastrous results. The King's wrath descended upon the hapless gardener and he was dismissed on the spot for gross negligence. The incident passed, a new growing season arrived and, lo and behold, the rose bed which had suffered the damage stood out from the rest as by far the best the royal household had ever seen. And so it became fashionable every autumn to heap all garden leaves and refuse adjacent to the beds so that the roses, which up until this time had been sacrosanct, could be burned by the devouring flames. The next step from this cumbersome, dangerous and not very effective method of pruning was to deliberately cut the wood with some sharp instrument.

Although rose species occurred naturally all over the Northern Hemisphere, we owe a great deal to the plant collectors of the last 200 years or so, some of whom endured all sorts of hardship to bring many of the types back to the Western world. Men like Robert Fortune—who was responsible for 'Fortune's Double Yellow' amongst others; George Staunton, William Kerr, and the early missionaries Fathers David, Hugo, Farges and Soulie. One of the most dedicated was Ernest Wilson, who collected roses from Western China; two well known roses he introduced are *R. willmottiae* and *R. moyesii*. Reginald Farrer is remembered for the 'Three-penny Bit Rose', *R. farreri persetosa*, and the Reverend Ernest Faber introduced the 'Wing Thorn Rose', *R. omeiensis pteracantha*.

R. laevigata was introduced into Europe in about 1696 and is known to be one of the most common roses in China. How long it has been growing there will never be known. It seems highly likely that this rose was taken to America long before that country's discovery by Christopher Columbus. No one will ever know whether it arrived when the two continents were still connected by land, or if it was taken there during the supposed discovery of North America by Chinese Monks, or whether the early Spaniards were responsible for its translocation. History has it that the first European explorers in the southern states found this rose well and truly established and took it to be a native American species, hence the common name 'Cherokee Rose'.

When paying tribute to early collectors of roses, we must make mention of the Empress Josephine. She was born Marie Josèphe Rose Tascher de la Pagere in 1763 on the island of Martinique. One wonders if the Rose in her given names was an omen for the future. Life on her home island was unkind to her. She married the Vicomte de Beauharnais in 1779 and lost him to the guillotine in 1794 during the revolution, and once free of all the encumbrances of her earlier unfortunate association, she married Napoleon Bonaparte in 1796. This was the opportunity she had been waiting for, to bury all her former

The beautiful alba, 'Josephine de Beauharnais'

sadness and disappointments and to achieve those grand designs which she had only dreamed of in her early life.

As Empress she was able to indulge all of her extravagant fancies. At her insistence, the gardens of Malmaison were extended to well over 1000 acres. As was fashionable among the nobility at the time, an English gardener (in fact a Scotsman in this case) was engaged to landscape the entire area, in accordance with the English Romantic Movement. The Empress saw to it that all 250 known varieties were collected for her gardens; no stone was left unturned to achieve this purpose. Her inspiration and popularity brought about a tremendous upsurge in rose culture and hybridisation so that from that time onwards both professionals and amateurs competed with each other to develop more and more varieties for people to love and admire.

History has established Josephine as the mentor and guide of Pierre-Joseph Redouté, who in turn is known as the painter of her roses. It is fitting that each in their own way has preserved for posterity the other's achievements.

It may be unknown to many of you that roses rate very highly in the language of flowers. A warm heart is represented by red and white roses, while a full blown rose means fleeting beauty. A rose without thorns means easy pleasure and a withered rose stands for beauty that has faded. The yellow rose symbolises infidelity and the moss rose is the sign of love and pleasure. The statue of silence holds a white rose in her hand and in ancient times it was commonplace for the doors of meeting and banqueting places to be garlanded with white roses to remind guests that as soon as they left the tables they should immediately forget all liberties and indiscretions. The Virgin Mary has had the Pompon rose or Rose of May, symbolising kindness, dedicated to her. Bengal or China roses, which can flower profusely throughout the year, are the emblems of willingness, and the Three Graces always wore a crown of roses with 100 petals. It is believed in some quarters that roses hold the key to dreams. Natural roses will bring wealth while artificial ones are reputed to bring evil. If you plan to give roses to someone as a gift for a special occasion a damask rose means 'bashful love'; the noisette 'Marechal Niel' means 'your heart and soul'; a musk rose means 'beauty'; a centifolia, 'agent of love'; and the species 'Austrian Copper', 'you are all that is lovely'.

The rose has been the emblem of beauty and grace in all ages. Its subtle fragrances, the elegance of its flowers and its many colours have meant that it has been loved and cherished and much sought after since the beginning of time.

The Hebrews of some 3000 years ago were known to have grown roses and frequent mention is made of them in most ancient holy writings. An ancient Arab author described the way to produce blue roses. It seems that indigo was dissolved in water and poured around the base of a white rose as the growth started and by the time the flowers arrived, they were a beautiful violet colour. The Greek poet Homer, and poetess Sappho, waxed lyrical about the rose. Anacreon too wrote in glowing terms about its beauty. It was believed in early times that the rose only became thorny after men became corrupt and learned evil ways. Herodotus writes of a double rose growing in the gardens of Midas, and early writers from the Orient sang the praises of the rose.

The sweat of the prophet Mahomet was the origin of the rose in Turkish legend and Imperial Rome dealt with the rose in sumptuous fashion — the Roman writers Horace, Virgil and Suetonius wrote much about roses, which were widely used in Roman celebrations. Such was the demand for rose flowers during these momentous times that production methods in Italy were stretched to the limit and flowers had to be brought in from Egypt. This never pleased the Roman rose-producers and it was not long before they had greatly improved their methods of growing and propagating to meet the needs of the period. In his writings, Pliny attempted classification of the roses of his time and was probably one of the first persons to do so.

During the Middle Ages the rose lost favour and religious establishments were probably responsible for its survival. The Moors successfully cultivated many rose varieties during the eleventh century using a number of methods. There were no recurrent varieties at this time. It is likely that the Moors were also the first to manufacture attar of roses in any quantity. Attar or rose oil was produced in many countries including France, England, China, Iran, India and Bulgaria, and many are the fanciful tales alluding to this particular product.

It was probably created in different places at different times, but legend has it that it was first discovered when an Emperor of Persia was walking with his princess quite close to a pool that had previously been strewn with scented rose petals. On observing an oily substance on the surface of the water, the princess knelt and scooped some of the liquid with her hand and was amazed at the delightful fragrance that came from it.

The rose has been used for medicinal purposes since very early times. 'The roses grown at Provins are conspicuous by their flower, their touch and their fragrance. They are more velvety and more brilliantly coloured: in preserves they are more unctuous, more resinous, and have a stronger and more agreeable odour,' wrote Dr Opoix in *L'Ancien Provins* (1805). The following extracts give an insight into the extensive use of roses by early herbalists. The medieval English has been translated into a modern form.

Ointment of Rose: 'Take four ounces of Rose Oil and one ounce of white beeswax, melt them together over boiling water then chafe them together with Rose water and a little vinegar.'
Treasury of Hidden Secrets (1586)

Damask Rose Syrup: 'Pour boiling water on a quantity of Damask Roses just enough to cover them. Let stand for twenty-four hours, then press off the liquor and add twice the quantity of sugar. Melt this and the syrup is completed.'
A Treatise of Cleanliness in Meats (1692)

Melrosette: 'Take fair purified honey and new red roses, the white ends of them clipped away, then chop them small and put into the honey and boil the mixture together; it is boiled enough when the red colour and sweet odour are at their best. Five years it may be kept in its virtue; by the roses he hath the virtue of comforting and by the honey he hath the virtue of cleansing.'
Banckes' Herbal (1525)

'*Honey of Roses* is much used in gargles and lotions to wash sores either in the mouth, throat or other parts, both to cleanse and heal them. '*Red Rose Water* is of familiar use on all occasions about the sick and of better use than Damask Rose Water, being cooling and cordial, refreshing and quickening the weak and faint spirits, either

used in meats or broths, to wash the temples, or to smell unto the nose or eke by the sweet vapours thereof out of a perfuming pot, or cast upon a hot fire shovel.
'Red Roses do strengthen the heart, the stomach and liver, and the retentive faculties; they mitigate the pains that arise from heat, assuage inflammation and procure sleep and rest.
'Electuary of Roses is purging and two or three drams of it taken in some convenient liquor is a competent purgation of any weak constitution, but may be increased unto six drams according to the quality and strength of the patient.
'Syrup of Dried Red Roses will strengthen a relaxed stomach, cooleth an overheated liver and the blood, comforteth the heart and resists putrefaction and infection.'   John Parkinson (1640)

Rose Drops: 'To a pound of sugar add an ounce of well beaten up rose petals and then wet with as much juice of lemon as will make it into a stiff paste; set it on a slow fire in a silver pot and stir well, and when it is scalding hot quite through, take it off and drop in small portions on a paper; place them near a fire, the next day they will come off.'   The Complete Housewife (1736)

During World War II tremendous efforts were made by the opposing sides to grow, harvest and process rose heps for the production of vitamin C which was almost unobtainable from the limited supply of oranges at the time. One hundred grams of oranges yields 50 milligrams of vitamin C, while the yield of vitamin C from 100 grams of Rosa rugosa fruit is over 3000 milligrams. From Mrs E. S. Rhodes's A Garden of Herbs:
Rose Hep Conserve: 'Take two pints of prepared rose hep puree and one pound of sugar; boil them together until a skin forms when poured on to a cold plate. Then pour into jars and seal immediately and store in a cool place.'
Rose Hep Marmalade: 'To every pound of heps take a half pint of water; boil until tender, strain the pulp through a sieve; to each pound of pulp add one pound of preserving sugar and boil until the mixture jellies.'
No discourse on roses would be complete without mention of potpourri. It seems that during the fourteenth century, the term had several meanings. A 'potpourri' could be a mixture of different meats; a combination of dried flowers and spices; or a musical or literary medley. Gradually it became most commonly connected with the mixing of fragrant rose petals, which were dried and stored. It is known that some of the ancient civilisations, such as the Greeks and the Romans, often used small sachets of scented petals and leaves as gifts

when entertaining. During the Great Plague of London in 1664-65, it was believed the infection could be combated by burning a mixture of frankincense, bay leaves, juniper twigs, rosemary and rose petals.
Although the nutritional and medicinal uses of the rose are not so widely recognised today, there is an upsurge in the popularity of sweetly fragrant potpourri. If you would like to make your own, try the following recipe.
You require dried rose petals from the varieties of your choice; extra dried flowers from plants other than roses; dried and crushed leaves from scented plants; dried lavender flowers; and small quantities of orange and lemon peel, nutmeg, cloves, allspice, and a pinch of salt. The rose petals should be plucked when just open, as this is the time the rose oil is at its strongest. They should be taken off the flower indoors and laid on clean white paper in a warm room. Mix all the ingredients thoroughly and leave for twenty-four hours, then slowly turn the mixture three or four times a day for about a week. The mixture can then be stored in a well sealed jar.

A corner of the display garden at Arowhenua

I suppose I will never cease to be amazed by the number of people and the diversity of occupations represented in those who take time out from the hurly-burly of modern-day life to drive in off the highway, step back in time and travel down through the years with our beautiful old roses in the display garden. One lovely balmy morning, when the scent from the roses was at its best, a gentleman and a lady drove into our parking area and one could not be blamed for thinking that they were a business couple just passing through. The man literally disappeared into the rose garden and after a while the lady began to look agitated. The situation worsened over the next hour or so until the lady made her way among the roses, obviously to tell her companion to hurry along. The man again showed reluctance to leave, as if he derived some hidden strength from being among the roses. Finally they moved back towards the car and all was explained. The gentleman was a High Court judge and the lady was his secretary: they were on their way to a nearby town for a court sitting. By this time they must have been at least half an hour late, but the gentleman remarked to his companion as they left, 'Well, they cannot start without me, can they?'

Autumn scene

Several years ago, an order came in by telephone for a group of assorted roses. No particular notice was taken of the name and address of the person who ordered them and a note was made that the plants would be collected on a certain day. The order was marked off from the stock numbers and in due time assembled and packaged for the designated day. About half of the working day had passed when a Land Rover arrived in the parking area and a gentleman alighted and announced that he had come for his bundle of roses. At that very moment I realised that I knew this man although I had never seen him before. Many years ago I had worked for his father, planting trees on the family farm, and here on my very doorstep was the son. He had lived the greater part of his life in England where he had reached the pinnacle of his career, serving his country and his Queen. He was astute enough to observe that the awareness of all this had just hit me. I did not know how to address him or what he would expect and he immediately put me at my ease by saying, 'Just call me Sam.' The gentleman concerned was Lord Elworthy, Marshal of the Royal Force, K.G., G.C.B., C.B.E., D.S.O., M.V.O., D.F.C., A.F.C., Former Chief of Staff of R.A.F., Former Chief Defence Staff, Constable and Governor of Windsor Castle.

One small group probably has a rather different reason for visiting the display garden. This group is made up of several school principals and teachers, both secondary and primary, who take time out from their various school duties, escape from the pressure of classroom and pupils and seek the solace of the scent and beauty of the roses, far from the pressures of the modern-day education system.

When dealing with visitors to our nursery and display garden I sometimes feel like helping them to enjoy their short stay by making them laugh or pulling their leg a little. The names of plants or roses and their history can often be used in this way. One day a lady whom I knew had four daughters arrived looking a little glum. We had sorted out the roses required and had adjourned to the office building where we were looking at some of the first colour proofs of the first volume of *The Book of Old Roses*. The full page plate of the alba 'Maiden's Blush' was being discussed when suddenly I could not resist cheekily asking the lady, 'Do maidens still blush?' As soon as I had asked the question, I had second thoughts about its propriety, but at last the answer came, amidst a lot of laughter: 'I'm damned sure they don't!'

One incident that happened a few years ago remains very vivid in my memory. It was a lovely early summer morning and my work at the time kept me near the parking area. Quite suddenly two cars carrying six ladies arrived, and for a moment one could be forgiven for trying to work out just what they represented and what the purpose of their visit was. They alighted from the rather official-looking cars, wearing jackets, trousers and knee boots which also looked semi-official. My first thoughts were that they could be an inquisitive police party out from Christchurch or even an Inland Revenue Department raid but when I recognised one of them the explanation was soon apparent. Old-rose lovers all of them, they had flown by Cessna aircraft from a town which was about 360 kilometres away, then taken two taxis to our place—and would have to repeat the journey on the way home. These old roses inspire people to do many things.

I hope that this meander through all sorts of subjects concerning the rose has been of some interest. We will now move on to Part Two, which includes a collection of some 600 roses with easy-to-read descriptions and as many colour plates as space and design allow. **As in the first volume the relevant piece of text is placed next to the colour plate for easy identification.**

Evangeline

PART TWO

The Roses

We seek for beauty on the height afar;
  But on the earth it glimmers all the while:
'Tis in the garden where the roses are;
  'Tis in the glory of a mother's smile.

E. W. Mason

Arvensis

Species and their Hybrids

Northern Hemisphere dwellers have enjoyed the particular pleasure derived from native roses not only over a great length of time but also over a vast area of countryside. But those who live in the Southern Hemisphere, though they are blessed with more than ample water supplies and hours of sunshine, are not endowed with native roses. For some inexplicable reason, when roses were created millions of years ago, the southern climates were not provided with any, whereas people in the northern continents enjoy the undoubted beauty of indigenous roses to this day. In New Zealand now there is *Rosa eglanteria (Rosa rubiginosa)* naturalised over hundreds of hectares, and anyone who has seen it in flower, smelled its green-apple fragrance and observed its magnificent display of fruit in the autumn will not easily forget the sight.

There are many indigenous rose species to be found in North America. One which excites comment is *R. stellata* and its form, 'Mirifica', the 'Sacramento Rose'. Its wide growing area extends over parts of New Mexico, Texas and Arizona, and its quite distinctive features can at times be seen from the roadside. It is a most unusual-looking rose, often referred to as the 'Gooseberry Rose'. It is extremely prickly and an upright grower when young, developing pendulous twisty growths with age.

A beautiful, distinctively different rose, *R. suffulta*, whose vast growing zone extends across the Great Plains region of Central North America, is another unusual example of exquisite beauty in a native rose, too beautiful to be called a persistent weed of the prairie wheat fields.

Crossing to the European continent, we pay a belated tribute to *R. gallica* and its forms which still grow wild in the countryside of many nations. This gentle, fertile, important member of the genus gave its talents unsparingly in so many ways and deserves the highest praise. It has been known under many different names and its true story has become fogged by time but its forms and descendants will live on.

R. persica is another very unusual rose, indigenous to parts of the Soviet Republic, Afghanistan and Iran, and able to survive in the driest possible conditions. It is true that its real name and classification is *Hulthemia* but as it is an ancestor of some hybrids and is still used in modern-day crosses, there is no harm in treating it as a rose. The flowers are the deepest yellow and about 3 to 4 cm across and have the deepest red blotch extending about a third of the length of the petal.

Travelling east, the native roses of China and Japan are many and varied. We owe a debt to this part of the world for the number of species that have found their way into our gardens and the profound effect they have had on many of our modern roses. Although records of roses in China are said to go back some 2000 years it would be true to say that, as in other countries, their real story will never be known.

Among the native roses of China is *R. filipes* whose strength, beauty and fragrance have to be seen and smelled to be believed. This beautiful species was introduced into Europe by that super-sleuth of plant collectors, E. H. Wilson.

Native to Japan is the unusual *R. roxburghii (R. microphylla)*, a not very well known rose that can be seen growing in the Emperor's Palace Garden in Tokyo. Its distinctive features include foliage that reminds one of gleditsia leaves, bark that peels from the older wood and very prickly fruit that resemble chestnuts, hence one of its common names.

This has been intentionally but a brief look at some native roses. Much can be written about them and indeed has been, but the true test comes when you decide to grow one or two of these historical treasures in your garden, requiring as they do plenty of garden room to develop and at the same time special room in your heart. ■

▲ **Andersonii** (1912). Single, bright pink flowers up to 7 cm adorn this graceful plant which can grow to 2 or more metres high and less than 2 metres wide. A good crop of fruit follows the flowering in mid summer. Probably a hybrid between *R. canina* and *R. arvensis*.

Arkansana (1917). Some pundits would have you believe that this species is the same as *R. suffulta* but this is not true. There are some similarities, but both the flowers and foliage of 'Arkansana' are larger than those of *R. suffulta*. It has single, pink flowers, 5 to 6 cm across. Grows to about 60 cm. Native to Kansas, Wisconsin and some other states.

▲ **Arvensis** 'Field Rose'. One of the oldest roses native to the British Isles and parts of Europe. A vigorous grower, but for all its strength it is at the same time very beautiful, with 5-cm, single, fragrant, creamy white flowers in summer followed by small, oval, bright red fruit. Distinctive hooked prickles.

Banksiae Hybride di Castello (1920). A very beautiful hybrid between *R. banksiae lutescens* and the noisette 'Lamarque'. It has pure white, large, double flowers and is a vigorous grower.

Banksiae Purezza (1961). An extremely beautiful Italian hybrid that looks as if it will become very popular. In warmer climates it has the ability to flower again later in the season. The 3-cm flowers in large clusters are double, fragrant and pure white. The growth is very vigorous and the light brownish young growths contrast nicely with the older green foliage.

Brunonii la Mortola (1954). A very fragrant form of the type which is extremely vigorous and has downy grey foliage. Clusters of large, pure white, single flowers in mid summer.

▲ **Californica Plena.** Very beautiful 10-cm semi-double flowers appear profusely on a rounded plant to about 2 metres. Blooms are a rich pink fading to lighter pink edges. Native to the western states of the United States.

Canina Vulgaris var. Transitoria 'Hildesheim Abbey Rose'. This rose has several medieval stories told about it. One popular legend has it that Emperor Ludwig had been out hunting and had become disorientated, losing his sense of direction. Deeply religious, he placed his crucifix and the ornate chain from which it was suspended on a nearby thorny shrub, and prayed for protection and guidance for his night alone. Next morning, searchers found him unharmed, sleeping peacefully beside a large rose plant. Such was the Emperor's gratitude for being delivered safely, he caused a chapel to be built on the spot and later it became the site of Hildesheim Abbey. Known affectionately as the 'Hildesheim Abbey Rose', this variety can be seen today growing in the courtyard of the abbey in West Germany.

The flowers, in large clusters, are medium-sized, single, white and fragrant. Can grow to 8 or more metres.

Carolina (1826). The state flower of Iowa, this rose is in fact native to a large area of the United States. Obviously, over such a wide-ranging environmental area there are variations, but my plant has bright pink, 5-cm, single flowers followed by bright red, round fruit. Its wood is quite prickly and the plant suckers quite freely.

▲ **Caudata** (1896). A fine species from China, growing to at least 5 metres. Single, scarlet flowers reminiscent of *R. moyesii* appear on the plant in groups of two or three. A distinctive rose in that the leaves have a slight scent and the 3-cm fruit are pear-shaped and orange-red in colour.

▲ **Centifolia Parvifolia** (1791) 'Burgundy Rose', 'Pompon de ·Burgoyne'. Upright plentiful growth with fine stems up to 60 cm high. Tight rosette flowers, 3 cm in diameter, sit upright on a healthy plant. The flower is wine-purple about the edge, paling in the centre.

▲ **Corymbifera** (1790). A single flower of about 8 cm across that is native to parts of Asia, Africa and Europe, and is believed to be a parent of *R. alba*. White with yellow stamens.

▲ **Chinensis**. It seems there will always be doubt about which rose should have this particular title, a small tribute to China, the country which has given us, either directly or indirectly, so many wonderful roses. The term 'Chinensis' has applied to many roses—in some cases it refers to semperflorens, and in others to suspected hybrids. Other synonyms are indica, odorata and sometimes gigantea.

▲ **Davidii Elongata** (1908). A more vigorously growing plant than the type. It has quite prickly wood but a graceful habit. The flowers and fruit are larger than *R. davidii*.
Davurica (1910). This not so common species has medium-sized, purplish pink, single flowers in mid summer followed by a good crop of oval fruit. Closely related to *R. cinnamomea*, possibly an Asian relative of that species.

▲ **Ecae** (1880) 'Afghan Rose'. A little beauty from Afghanistan that forms a delightful small shrub, 90 to 120 cm high. Its pendulous branches are covered with dainty, fern-like foliage and a profusion of deep yellow, single flowers, about 3 cm across, sitting upright. Not easy to propagate but well worth the trouble it might take.

▲ **Eglanteria Magnifica.** A very beautiful hybrid which, when in flower, is choked with its profusion of blooms. They are a little more than single, white in the centre and rosy red towards the edges. Has the usual attributes of the parent.

▲ **Fenja** (1908). A distinctive hybrid from *R. davidii* and *R. spinosissima* raised by Valdemar Petersen of Denmark. It has single, medium-sized, bright pink flowers which are strongly fragrant. Makes an attractive tall shrub. Beautiful fruit.

Filipes (1908). This species has very large clusters of very fragrant, pure white, single flowers which are 3 cm or so in diameter. A native of Western China that has the ability to thrive under poor conditions. Grows to about 3 metres.

▲ **Filipes Brenda Colvin** (1970). A very vigorous hybrid which is notable for its single, very fragrant, 3-cm flowers which appear in large clusters. They are blush-pink in colour and contrast nicely with the dark, shiny foliage.

Foliolosa (1880). This North American species has single, blush flowers about 4 cm across. Flowering time early to mid summer, blooms usually appear singly. Bright red, rounded fruit.

▲ **Golden Chersonese** (1967). A very beautiful hybrid from *R. ecae* and 'Canary Bird'. A compact plant with a profusion of 5-cm, deep yellow, single, fragrant flowers.

▲ **Helenae Hybrida.**
This hybrid can be delightful when grown up trees or tall buildings. It can easily reach 6 or 7 metres, and has one exuberant display in mid summer. Almost single flowers, beautifully fragrant, are creamy yellow at first with orange stamens.

▲ **Hemisphaerica** 'Sulphur Rose'. A very important old rose which was introduced into Western Europe from Asia about the middle of the seventeenth century. It grows tall to about 2.5 metres, and has very double, bright yellow, 5-cm flowers. One sad point about it is that although plentiful, fat, greenish yellow buds are provided, they open successfully only in a hot, dry climate.

Hemsleyana (1904). This species from central China can be expected to grow to at least 2 metres. Its display of single, light pink, 5-cm flowers in mid summer is followed by oval, 3-cm fruit, which are distinctive because of their long necks.
Horrida (1796). An interestingly different type from Southern Europe and Asia Minor. It develops into a small, prickly bush, about 60 cm high, with white flowers that are followed by small, rounded, dark red fruit.
Kochiana (1869). Bright green foliage makes this hybrid attractive, especially in contrast to the 4-cm, single, purple-pink flowers. Quite prickly branches.
Luciae Onoei. This rose seems to be a smaller version of *R. wichuraiana*. It is low-growing with small, shiny, bright green leaves and single, white, fragrant flowers about 2 cm across.

Moyesii Rosea *R. holodonta*. This species, like the type, comes from China. Light pink, single flowers and flagon-shaped fruit. Grows to 3 metres.

▲ **Moyesii Superba** (1950). A beautiful, deep red hybrid which has the usual attributes of this family, except that the flowers are semi-double rather than single.

▲ **Macrantha Daisy Hill** (1906). An important rose because of its contribution to the creation of new roses. It has very attractive, large, fragrant, almost single, pink flowers followed by a fine crop of round, red fruit. Will grow to more than 3 metres.

Macrophylla (1818). This native of the Himalayas will grow to 3 metres high. After the 5-cm, single, red flowers appear in groups of up to three, beautiful, elongated, bristly, red fruit adorn the plant.

Manetti. This hybrid was raised by Dr Manetti in about 1837 while he was associated with the Milan Botanical Garden in Italy. 'Manetti' or its relatives, such as 'Lippiat's Manetti' in New Zealand, have been widely used as understocks.

Micrugosa Walter Butt (1954). A more recent hybrid which has large, single, deep pink flowers, 10 cm or more across. Its fruit resembles that of its parent.

Minutifolia (1882) 'Tiny Leaf Rose'. A rare species from the lower California area. The plant can reach a height of between 60 and 90 cm and likes a hot dry climate. The foliage, which is greyish green, is deeply lacinated and the 2.5-cm, single flowers can be white or pale pink. Small, bristly, round, red fruit. Altogether a distinctive rose.

▲ **Moyesii Fred Streeter** (1951). A hybrid from *R. moyesii*. Single, pinkish red flowers adorn the plant in the usual manner and are followed by the flagon-shaped fruit typical of this family.

Multibracteata (1904). E. H. Wilson, that master of plant collectors, was responsible for the introduction of this fine species from the valley of the River Min in China. Grows to 2 metres with 3-cm, single, pink flowers followed by a bounteous crop of oval, reddish orange fruits.

Multiflora. When the French engineer Coignet sent seeds of a rose to the mayor of Lyon in 1862, he little knew what a wonderful rose *R. multiflora* would prove to be. Not only did this important species pass·on many of its attributes to its offspring among the polyanthas, floribundas and ramblers, but it became, and in fact still is, an important root-stock used in many countries. Its adaptability is shown in its use for anything from 3-metre weeping standards in Japan, to an impenetrable barrier on freeway entrances and median strips in the United States, to the base for miniature roses in Denmark. From the nurseryman's point of view, *R. multiflora* and many of its forms are excellent stock to work with—comparatively thornless, upright growing and able to make roots easily from cuttings. Altogether an extremely useful rose, and perhaps it will be taken up again by hybridists looking for improvement and change in present-day roses. The type has single, small, very fragrant, white flowers in clusters and the plant grows to at least 3 metres. It is native to parts of China, Korea and Japan.

Multiflora Cathayensis (1907). Differing from the previous species in its larger, 5-cm, single, bright pink flowers. Overall, a less vigorous plant.

▲ **Palustris** (1726) 'Swamp Rose'. This species, as its common name implies, prefers damp soil conditions. It will remain short in stature in dry ground, but will grow tall to 2 metres or more in its favoured areas. Deep pink, 5-cm flowers from mid summer.

▲ **Persica** (1788) *R. berberifolia*, 'Hulthemia persica'. Fragrant, deep yellow flowers, 3 to 4 cm across, with a deep red eye extending about a third of the length of the petal. Simple grey-green leaves, prickly fruit that withers rather than colours, and bicoloured stems. Has come into its own in recent years because of its use by modern hybridists as a parent in crosses with modern roses. I have had the pleasure of seeing some of the beautiful first- and second-generation seedlings in the Harkness glasshouses at Hitchin in England. They have retained most of the features of their famous parent but, influenced by their other more modern parent, the flowers have become fully double, rather like double ranunculus flowers, and they also retain the distinctive red eye to a greater or lesser degree. It is not in my province to hazard a guess as to the future generations of *R. persica* when seedlings from these crosses finally produce flowers and they are unveiled to our eyes in the years to come. *R. persica* can only be increased from seed and it seems best for it to be sown where the plant is to be permanently established. Its obsolete name, *R. berberifolia*, refers to its barberry-like foliage.

Phoenicia. A species of great antiquity and of great importance. Native to Asia Minor, it is believed to have been introduced into Europe in 1885. It is a near relative of *R. moschata*, but it is less hardy and vigorous. The flowers are pure white, 5 cm in diameter, single and produced in panicles.

▲ **Pomifera** (1771) *R. villosa*, 'Apple Rose'. Native to Northern Europe and parts of Asia. It gets its common name from the fruit but they are more gooseberry-like in appearance. Flowers are bright rose-pink and the foliage is greyish green. Height up to 2 metres.

The Book of Classic Old Roses

▲ **Roxburghii** *(R. microphylla)*.
This is a beautiful species,
unusual in several ways, with
holly-like foliage; large,
single, pale pink flowers,
paling towards their centres;
chestnut-like fruit; bark which
peels; and a pair of dark red
prickles at the base of each
leaf stem.

►**Serafinii** (1914). A species
that is closely related to *R.
eglanteria*. It has quite small,
pink, single flowers and the
plant grows to about 1 metre.
Its natural habitat is the
Mediterranean area.

Sericea. There seems to be some confusion between this species and *R. omeiensis*. My plant appears to be finer than the latter in every way. They both have white, single, four-petalled flowers which, although fleeting, are quite beautiful, and they both have small scarlet fruit—but there the similarity ends.

Sericea Heather Muir (1957). This hybrid will reach up to 3 metres and has large, four-petalled, pure white flowers over a long season, followed by attractive orange-red fruit.

Setipoda (1895). Three metres is the approximate height of this beautiful species. It is a native of central China and has very pretty, 5-cm, rose-pink single flowers followed by red, pear-shaped, large fruit. Attractive ferny foliage which is sweet-brier scented.

Sinowilsoni (1904) 'The Wilson Rose'. A very vigorous and beautiful species climber that has glossy green, large foliage, wine-purple beneath. It can be damaged by cold weather. Has smallish white flowers, about 4 cm across, which appear in large loose heads.

▲ **Spaldingii** (1915). Single pure white flowers with lemon-yellow stamens, followed by profuse, rounded, small, red fruit. Native to many areas of North America.

Spinosissima Hispida (1781). Soft, sulphur-yellow, 6- to 8-cm single flowers on a plant which reaches 1.5 metres. Forms a compact plant with many bristles.

Spinosissima Minima. A rare dwarf form, this lovely, small compact plant, about 30 cm high, has single, white flowers with black stamens.

Spinosissima Mrs Colville. Another beautiful member of the family that has purplish crimson, almost single flowers with white centres and yellow stamens.

▲ **Spinosissima Myriacantha** (1820). This plant's native habitat spreads across parts of Spain and France. Has very prickly compact growth, small white flowers and blackish fruit.

Stellata (1897) 'Gooseberry Rose'. Probably a very old rose, a native of New Mexico. It has 5-cm, single, purplish pink flowers followed by dullish red, bristly, pear-shaped fruit. Height about 1 metre. Most successful way to increase it is from seed.

Stellata Mirifica (1916) 'Sacramento Rose'. A larger, hardier version of the previous rose, also a native of New Mexico. Height about 1.5 metres.

▼▲ **Suffulta** (1880). Native to the Great Plains area of the United States. Forms a very prickly small shrub of about 45-50 cm with single, 4-cm, pink flowers. Unusual in that it can flower on both old and new wood. Large, red, rounded fruit and fern-like foliage.

The Book of Classic Old Roses

▲ **Tomentosa** (1820). Believed to be a hybrid between *R. canina* and *R. mollis* and shows some affinity to *R. pomifera*. Grows tall to 2 metres or more and has bright greyish green foliage, pink 4-cm flowers and smallish, reddish, rounded fruit.

Turkestanica (1900). A little-known rose from the Turkestan area which is possibly related to *R. spinosissima*. It has pale yellow single flowers which appear singly or in groups of two or three. An interesting and different species.

◄▲ **Virginiana** (1724). One of the most beautiful roses of any family. A rounded plant of about 1.5 metres, it has glossy green leaves that always look healthy; 5-cm, single, pink flowers, quite bright; very bright red, rounded fruit which last long after the foliage has dropped; and foliage that puts on one of the brightest displays of any deciduous shrub in the plant world. Praise indeed but it deserves it. Native to a wide area of Eastern North America.

Wichuraiana Potereriifolia. A little-known variety of the type which is smaller than its parent in every way. It has small twiggy growth, single, small, fragrant, white flowers and glossy green foliage.

Wichuraiana Variegata. Another not so well known variety of the parent type, quite beautiful in its own way. The foliage is variegated, creamy and glossy green, with pink on the youngest growth. Single, white fragrant flowers.

Wintonensis (1935). Recognised as a hybrid of *R. moyesii* and *R. setipoda* and has the sweet-brier fragrance of the latter. The flowers are very bright cerise-pink and the fruit is orange-red.

Perle des Panachées

Gallicas and their Hybrids

Leaving behind the species and their relatives, most likely the start of it all, it seems just as certain that the gallicas were the next in the line of succession. This family has given much to the roses that came later. As a group they were and are superlative. I never cease to be amazed at the number of these magnificent roses that are still available, and the group described hereafter have just as many attributes as any that we may have known before, with unique colours, upright and usually compact growth, striped varieties which are more numerous than in other groups, and, above all, fragrance second to none.

Because of its ability to produce seed which germinates freely, and an inbuilt hardiness that enables it to survive under the most difficult conditions, this group became widespread across many countries. It has been recognised under different names and the confusion was probably added to by the title 'Red Damask' that was used in England over a long period of time. This reputedly came about by the rose being brought back from the Crusades.

Some 167 varieties of gallicas were listed in the Empress Josephine's collection up until 1814, and history has it that such people as Joan of Arc, Emperor Napoleon and Henry II received gifts made from the 'Apothecary's Rose' when visiting the French city of Provins. Pliny wrote about the 'Rose of Miletus' as bearing red blossoms of extreme brilliance which apparently had twelve petals, and although no evidence exists to prove or disprove its identity it seems likely to have been a gallica.

It is recorded that

Descemet, a Frenchman, was the first to breed roses in any great number. When Descemet's plants were threatened by the forces opposing Napoleon, Vibert, his fellow countryman, rescued some 10,000 seedlings, most of which were gallicas. It is perhaps fitting that many Frenchmen were responsible for the development of the early gallicas, among them what were to become famous names, such as Prevost, Laffay, Dupont, Lelieur and Desportes.

The striped, spotted and variegated flowers, which are more predominant in this family than any other, sometimes provoke quite adverse reactions, partly due to an incorrect assumption that the remarkable colour variations were caused by a virus or infection. Extensive scientific testing has laid this misapprehension firmly to rest—the variations are natural and healthy and including striped and variegated forms in your rose garden therefore becomes simply a matter of taste. The variegated forms are becoming more popular and there are many new variations, including delightful striped miniature roses. It could be said that liking striped roses is an acquired taste, much the same as eating kiwifruit or cucumber, but once you appreciate their benign beauty you will surely become hooked on their charms and will probably return to their festive table for more and more.

The roses described in this section lose nothing in comparison to those in the first volume, in fact this group is even better because it contains the very rare white gallica, 'Comtesse de Lacépède'. ∎

▲ **Adèle Heu** (1816) 'Duc d Orleans'. Upright, medium growth. Double, fragrant flowers of bright purplish pink.

▲ **Adèle Prevost** (1848). Cupped flowers, soon reflexing, leaving centre petals erect. A strong-growing plant of pink to light red. Double and fragrant.

▲ **Aimable Amie** (1860). Deep pink, double flowers which are fragrant. The plant is tall growing and the flowering prolific.

The Book of Classic Old Roses

▲ **Boule de Nanteuil** (1848).
A very beautiful gallica which
has large, very double, deep
pink, fragrant flowers with
silvery shades on the outside.
Comte de Nanteuil (1852). A
seedling from 'Boule de
Nanteuil' which has very
large 10-cm or more flowers.
The colour is purplish
crimson with fiery crimson
centres and the plant is wide
and branching.

▲ **Aimable Rouge** (1845). A
beautiful rose with fragrant,
medium-sized, double, pink
to red flowers. A medium to
tall grower.

▲ **Belle Doria**. Deep violet,
well-filled, double flowers
growing to medium height.
Some white spots appear at
times.

▲ **Bouquet de Venus**. An
extremely pretty rose of pale
blush-pink, double and
quartered. Strong scent.

▲ **Comtesse de Lacépède** (1848).
Although this beautiful rose
has some centifolia blood in
it, it would appear to be the
best white gallica. It has very
double, quartered, white,
fragrant flowers with a green
pointel. Quite distinctive.

Conditorum. A very beautiful rose which is semi-double and large, about 10 cm or more. The colour is purplish red with some of the golden stamens showing. Very fragrant.

Cosimo Ridolfi (1842). Compact growth with very double, medium-sized, lilac-rose flowers with spots of crimson. Unusual and beautiful.

Duchesse de Berry (1825). Strongly scented, deep pink, large flowers on a tall plant. Beautiful but not so well known.

Daphné (1819). A lovely pink member of the group. It has medium-sized, double, fragrant flowers that adorn a tall-growing plant.

Fanny Bias (1819). Large, double flowers of perfect form, blush-pink with deeper centres, on an upright plant. Very fragrant.

Gloire des Jardins. This variety has purple-red, medium-sized, double flowers on a medium-sized plant. Quite distinctive and fragrant.

Gros Provins Panaché. Unusual, with lovely, violet-purple, double flowers that have white streaks through the petals. Grows to about 1.5 metres. Fragrant.

▲ **Henri Fouquier** (1854). Extremely beautiful, a compact grower to about 1 metre. It is fragrant, very double, the purest pink and also almost thornless.

▲ **Ipsilanté** (1821). A rose of rare distinction that ought to become better known. Large, double flowers of the prettiest pale lilac-pink, quartered and fragrant. Medium growth.

▲ **La Louise** (1840). Unusual in that its purplish red, semi-double flowers lighten to cream at the base. Tall growing and fragrant.
La Neige. Not to be confused with the moss rose of the same name. Double, white and fragrant. A beautiful rose.

◄**Louis Philippe** (1824) 'Grandissima'. There is a china rose with this name. This rose has very large, rosy crimson and purplish flowers that are double and fragrant. Medium-sized plant with spreading habit.

▲ **Mme d'Hébray** (1820). The base colour of these lovely, double, fragrant flowers is white, with pink and light red stripes running through them.
◄**Marcel Bourgouin** (1899). If you want success with this rose then it requires extra attention with extra food and water. Unusual combination of velvety deep reddish purple, mottled violet.
Mécène (1845). A medium-sized, double flower, white with lilac-pink stripes. Upright grower and almost thornless.

The Book of Classic Old Roses

▲ **Nanette.** A pretty crimson double flower in clusters on a plant up to 1.5 metres. Blooms are sometimes veined and streaked.

▲ **Nestor** (1840). Beautiful light red and magenta shadings contrast nicely with the light green leaves of this medium-sized plant. Almost thornless.

▲ **Oeillet Flammand** (1845). Do not confuse this rose with the damask of the same name. A very double rose, striped in a pretty way with rose-pink and lilac.
Oeillet Parfait (1841). It seems that we cannot get away from striped roses in this family. This variety has rosy crimson stripes on a double, white, fragrant flower.

▲ **Ornament de la Nature** (1826) 'Anemone Ancienne'. Rare rose of distinctive beauty. Medium-sized, double flower, of lilac- to violet-pink. Tall growing.

▲ Perle des Panachées (1845). There is also a centifolia with this name. Distinct rose-pink stripes on a white, double flower. Upright growth.

► Petite Orléanaise (1845). A very beautiful rose of light clear pink with rosette form and button centres. The plant will grow to about 1.5 metres and could be used for a pillar. Lightly scented flowers are about 8 to 9 cm across.

Prince Frédéric (1840). Very double, large, red, fragrant flowers on a tall-growing plant. A fine variety.

Reine des Amateurs (1845). A very good variety with deep lilac-pink flowers that are very double, full and fragrant. Tall-growing plant.

Rouge Admirable (1825). Another fine variety. Tall growing, with medium fragrance and double, purple-red, well-shaped flowers.

◄ Ville de Londres. This variety is not so well known but it is well worth having just the same. Double, medium-sized flowers which are cerise-pink and fragrant. Compact growth.

Bella Donna

Damasks and their Hybrids

Traditionally this family has been credited with containing the best-scented roses of all, even though roses from other families may have good fragrances. The use of damask roses for the distillation of attar for expensive perfumes and cosmetics has contributed to their reputation for beautiful fragrance. We are well aware of the fields of damask roses for attar in Kazanlik in Bulgaria, but the fields in Morocco, Algeria, Egypt, Israel, India, France and Turkey are perhaps not so well known.

When thinking of the rose fields in Egypt, I am reminded of a neighbour of mine. A very proficient breaker and trainer of horses, he had one horse that showed particular aptitude and learned all sorts of tricks. As the First World War developed, many horses, including some of his, were commandeered by the New Zealand Army for action overseas. My neighbour was attached to the infantry and was on his way to the fighting zone in Europe when his unit stopped for a break and training session somewhere south of Cairo. While making his way to that city for a short spell of leave with friends, he passed a cavalry unit near some fields of damask roses. Horses were always his interest and the group had to inspect the animals row upon row. Imagine the amazement of all present when my neighbour recognised his favourite horse and very soon had him performing his routine of tricks. The haunting fragrance of damask roses always reminded my neighbour of that incredible coincidence all those years ago.

The roses of this group are singularly beautiful and stand apart from the other families. Because of their strength of growth and light green foliage, they are ideal plants to use between other roses and all types of ornamental shrubs. The early members of the family are of great antiquity so have the ability to flower only once in each summer season, but I would remind the reader that your favourite camellia, rhododendron or azalea flowers only once in each season too! ■

Bella Donna. Large double flowers on a branching plant to about 1 metre. Very fragrant lilac-pink flowers. A fine variety.

Bernard (1846). A tall-growing, very fragrant variety with deep pink, medium-sized, double flowers.

Catherine Ghislaine (1885). A neat, medium-growing plant which has small semi-double flowers, white with violet-purple stripes.

Césonie (1859). This variety makes a rounded compact plant and has the prettiest deep pink flowers. Fragrant.

Déeseflore. One of the most prolific flowerers of the family. Almost white, small to medium flowers, with pinkish centres, appear on a medium-sized plant.

▲ **Duc de Sussex.** Creamy white and pink, large, double, fragrant flowers grace a tallish plant of about 1 metre or more.

Léon Lecomte (1854). Pinkish red with lemon at the base of the petals. Large, double, fragrant flowers on a tallish plant.

Louis Cazas (1850). Not so well known. Medium-sized deep pink flowers which are very double and have a medium scent. Tallish plant.

▲ **Crimson Damask.** One of the few single damask roses. Medium- to large-sized flowers of carmine and purplish red. Fragrant.

▲ **Oratam** (1939). This more modern hybrid introduces new colours into the family. The flowers are coppery pink with lemon at the base and on the reverse of the petals, and they are large, double and very fragrant.

Phoebus. Large, very double, lilac-blush flowers with deeper centres. Upright growth and fine foliage.

Professor Emile Perrot (1930). Very strongly scented, semi-double, medium-sized flowers of deep pink. Upright growth to about 1.5 metres.

Roi des Pays-Bas. Beautiful deep red, large, double, fragrant flowers on a medium to tall plant. Not so common.

Rose a Parfum de Bulgarie. This rose, which is not very

well known, originated in Kazanlik, east of Sophia in Bulgaria. Strongly scented, double, medium-sized flowers which are rose-pink.

Rose a Parfum de Grasse. This rose is similar to the above in that it is strongly scented and has double, medium-sized, rose-pink flowers.

▲ **Rose d'Hivers**. An extremely interesting rose which is probably of great age. Quite small flowers, pink in the bud opening to pure white. Nicely double and fragrant.

Rosier de Damas (1840). Double, medium-sized, pink flowers grace a tidy plant to about 1 metre. Fragrant.
Sémiramis (1841). An unusual rose which has glossy pink flowers with almost fawn centres. The flowers are large and very double, and, of course, fragrant.
Van Huysum. Medium-sized, double, pink flowers grace a compact tidy plant to 1 metre. Fragrant.

A Feuilles de Chanvre

Albas and their Relatives

These distinctive roses, with their subtle colours and elusive fragrance, are documented from at least 2000 years ago and have been prominent in gardens ever since. They have been painted by many artists including Pierre-Joseph Redouté and a number of the Italian Renaissance masters.

The alba group were taken to heart by the English, much as the gallicas were by the French. The House of Lancaster adopted the red rose (probably a form of *R. gallica*) as its emblem and the House of York adopted a white rose. Historically it is generally believed that the alba 'Semi-plena' was the 'White Rose of York'. During what were romantically called the Wars of the Roses, these two members of the genus *Rosa* assumed great significance. So much so that when Henry VII, a Lancastrian, married Elizabeth of York, the two roses were symbolically merged into one that became known as the 'Tudor Rose'. This emblem is still used by members of the Royal Family today and appears on the coins of England.

I wonder if there is anything significant in the fact that the Royal National Rose Society of England has established a magnificent rose garden at St Albans in the very area where the first battle of the Wars of the Roses took place in 1455. Perhaps some deep-seated and inexplicable force was responsible for this amazing coincidence, perhaps not.

Typical features of this family include a scent that has been likened to that of white hyacinths, lightly thorned or sometimes thornless wood, greenish grey foliage, and white, cream, blush or pink flowers on upright plants. As far as I have observed, none of them can send up any late flowers. ∎

▲ **A Feuilles de Chanvre**. A very lovely double, white, fragrant member of the group. Compact growth to about 1 metre.

Beauté Virginale. A rose that is beautiful in its simplicity. Double, white, medium-sized and fragrant.
Belle Aurore. Quite a large flower which is very double and flesh-pink in colour with darker shadings. Greyish green foliage.

▲ **Blanche de Belgique** (1817) 'Blanche Superbe'. Compact, double, white flowers of medium to large size. It has a good scent and the usual greyish green foliage.

▲ **Armide** (1817). This variety, although one of the older ones in this family, loses nothing in comparison with any of the others. Beautiful pink and white, double, medium-sized, fragrant flowers adorn a plant to a little over 1 metre.

Esmaralda (1847). Again beautiful in its simplicity, with double, medium-sized, attractive flowers of flesh-pink fading to white at the edges.
Etoile de la Malmaison. Similar to the previous rose in that it has double, flesh-pink flowers fading to white at the edges but they are larger. Also the plant grows taller and more erect.
►**Josephine de Beauharnais**. It is fitting that this beautiful rose should be named after a beautiful lady. The plant is medium and erect and has attractive dark green foliage. The flowers are palish pink with blush edges and are cupped, of medium size and fragrant.

▲ **Blush Hip** (1840). A strong-growing member of the family. Flowers early in the season. Classic form with medium-sized flowers of light blush-pink, deeper pink in the centre.

▲ **Carnea-Incarnata** (1557). A very beautiful rose, typical of the family, with double, light pink flowers in profusion. Fragrant.

Cuisse de Nymphe Émue (1802). Some enthusiasts would have it that this rose is the same as 'Great Maiden's Blush', and others are just

as sure that it is not. Beautifully fragrant, with greyish leaves and sumptuous, blush-pink flowers.

▲ **Ménage** (1847). There is no shortage of beautiful roses in this group, this one being another example. Palest pink, medium-sized, double, fragrant flowers bloom profusely on a compact plant.

▼ **Minette** (1819). Light pink fragrant flowers, double and beautiful in form, grace a medium-sized plant. This rose is a good example of a variety which became well known in a country different from its origin and under a local name. The country is Sweden and its adopted name is 'Suionum'.

▲ **Sappho** (1817). An exquisite rose, white and almost single. It has good fragrance and the upright plant grows to over 1 metre high. The flowers are medium sized.

Victorine la Couronnée (1845). An unusual and beautiful rose, light pink with red stripes. Lightly scented flowers are nicely double, appearing on a medium-sized plant.

Unica Alba

Centifolias and their Hybrids

The distinguishing features of this group include deeply serrated handsome foliage; prickles that are usually unequal, whether large or small; delicious fragrance; a pendulous or branching habit; and globular flowers. As more examples of this family become available it becomes very apparent that there is a great diversity of origins within this family with hybrids from a number of groups including the chinas, and some quite small varieties. It is not my intention to add any confusion to an already difficult subject by dividing them again — for all practical purposes the heading used for this section is admirable.

Some months ago, a letter arrived for me from a lady in Meldorf, West Germany, asking me to identify what was thought to be a centifolia rose, and a colour photograph was included. Because of the widespread interest created by my first volume, *The Book of Old Roses*, many such letters arrive from all parts of the world, just proving that there is tremendous interest in these old beauties.

In 1984 I made a long wished-for journey through a number of Northern Hemisphere countries to visit people and places with whom considerable contacts had been made over many years. Over Easter weekend I travelled from Leipzig to Frankfurt and from Trier to Hamburg. I had no appointments on Easter Monday, so decided to visit Westerland. After travelling some way I realised the train would pass through Meldorf so it seemed a good idea to try to contact the lady who had sent me the centifolia inquiry. I walked from the railway to Klaus Groth Strasse and luckily found the lady at home.

A most pleasant afternoon followed and of course old roses and their identification was the main topic of conversation. We visited the local museum, the director of which just happened to be the lady's husband, and saw the treasures rescued from much earlier days. A most memorable day finished with a delightful meal in a local restaurant. My, by now, good friends said *'Auf wiedersehen'* at the station and remarked what a very rosy and happy Easter it had been for them. Our meeting was evidence of the special bond between old-rose lovers throughout the world. ∎

Ballady (1934). A recent hybrid which is medium pink and double. The plant grows to about 1 metre. A fine addition to the family.

▲ **Blanchefleur** (1835). One of the treasures of the group. It performs well in our climate. Large, very double flowers, about 10 cm across, are quartered, quite flat, and creamy white with touches of blush-pink. Sweetly scented.
Blue Boy (1958). A more recent hybrid from the house of Kordes. The very strongly scented double flowers are an unusual violet-red colour. The plant reaches about 1 metre.

Chou 'Rose Chou'. This very old variety forms a compact, rounded plant of more than 1 metre. Its medium-sized pink flowers are fragrant and of great beauty.
Ciudad de Oviedo *R. centifolia simplex*. A rose classified by Thory that seems to have a mixed history. Its beauty lies in the simplicity of its single pink flowers.

▲ **Decora**. One of the small-flowering members of the group. The flowers are very double, slightly scented and the compact plant will gradually reach about 1 metre.
Descemet. A very old and beautiful rose. The exquisite flowers, which are large and double, are an even, medium pink, paling a little with age. A very fine rose.

▲ **Duc de Brabant** (1857). Light red, medium-sized, double flowers adorn a healthy upright plant. Not to be confused with 'Duchesse de Brabant', a tea rose.
Duc de Fitzjames (1885). The plant is of medium height and the double flowers are a pretty, light purple-red. An excellent rose, not so well known.

The Book of Classic Old Roses

▲ **Foliacée** (1810) 'Caroline de Berri'. A compact grower with pleasant, medium-sized flowers of light pink. An old variety but a useful one.

▲ **Provence Pink**. A beautiful rose of soft, light pink. Flowers are of medium size and quite double. The branching plant makes moderate growth to about 1 metre.

▲ **Reine de Saxe**. A little-known centifolia rose, light pink in colour. It has a good scent and the flowers are double and of medium size. The upright plant will grow to 1 metre or more.

▲ **Prolifera de Redouté**. This rose is of great age and is also very beautiful. Its lovely pale rose-pink flowers are quite double and are cupped with frilled petals. Strong fragrance.

▲ Rose des Peintres (1800) 'Rose von Batavia'. A tall-growing older member of the group. Strongly scented, very double, medium-sized, bright pink flowers.

►Unica Alba (1775) 'Unique Blanche', 'White Provence'. This rose is indeed unique. A very beautiful creamy white, at times translucent. The flowers are strongly fragrant, of medium size and, compared to other members of the group, arrrive late in the season.

Unique Panachée (1821). Of all the striped roses in all the families, and there are many, this may be one of the prettiest. The flowers are white and, under favourable conditions, have pretty pink stripes.

◄Variegata (1845). 'La Rubanee' is sometimes given this name. This rose is mainly white or creamy, with fine stripes of pink. It is fragrant and grows to about a metre or more. An excellent variety.

James Veitch

Mosses and their Hybrids

This family will always be singularly different from all others in that it is the only group to have originated by sporting or mutation and not from seed as in all other groups. After the arrival of moss roses on the scene it was not long before hybridists began creating other types, and hybrids are recognised today from gallicas, damasks and hybrid chinas. Much later, some climbing mosses arrived and it seems that 'Wichmoss' is the only one to survive.

Ralph Moore of Visalia, California has recently accomplished much with dwarf, striped and climbing moss roses. He is known throughout the world for his pioneering work with miniature roses (as you are reminded when you see the number plate of his car, which reads WEE ROSE) and he has used his remarkable skill to create a number of miniature moss roses, both single and double. He has also developed a large group of very distinctive striped moss roses, as well as a number of striped and plain climbing mosses. It is my fervent hope that his climbing mosses will eventually find their way into our gardens, not only because of their unusual beauty but also because a large number of them have the ability to flower later in the season.

Mosses need the best of growing conditions as some are very delicate. Do not be concerned if your moss roses have flowers of a different colour or even a different form on the one plant—it is natural that the process by which they were created is sometimes reversed. ■

Angelique Quetier (1839). Quite old, this variety has purplish pink, very double, medium-sized flowers and a light scent.

Asepala. An unusual rose in that the edges of the petals are curled. The flowers are small, quite double and basically white with a flesh shading, sometimes having much deeper edges.

Black Boy. Very beautiful dark red flowers are of medium size, very double and they have a strong fragrance.

Blanche Simon (1862). One of the few white moss roses that do well under most conditions. Not very well known. Fragrant, medium-sized, double flowers.

▲ **Célina** (1855). Deep red flowers grace a tallish plant of more than 1 metre. Medium-sized, double and fragrant.

▲ **Capitaine Basroger** (1890). This variety may have a few late flowers. Tall-growing, thorny plant of about 2 metres has purplish crimson, cupped flowers of medium size.

▼ **Coralie** (1860). There is a damask with this name. This variety has medium-sized, very double, pink flowers with white shadings. Has a pleasing fragrance.

The Book of Classic Old Roses

◄**Duchesse d'Abrantes** (1851). Raised in the same year and by the same breeder, the Frenchman Robert, as 'D'Arcet'. Beautiful, double, fragrant pink flowers, shaded white.

▼ Duchesse de Verneuil (1856). Like the reds, good pink moss roses, such as this one, are not so common. An upright, healthy plant with fragrant bright pink flowers which have paler undersides.

▲ Crimson Globe (1890). Raised in England, this beautiful member of the group is perhaps not so well known. It has large, very double, rounded, deep crimson flowers.

▲ D'Arcet (1851). There was a time when pink moss roses were not common but this is no longer so. This French-raised member of the group is well worth a place in any garden. Double, medium-sized, fragrant flowers.

►Dresden Doll (1975). One of three small-flowering recent moss roses raised by Ralph Moore. Soft pink, cupped, fragrant, small, semi-double flowers. Repeat flowering.

Emilie. Small, double flowers of pure white appear on a medium-sized plant. Fragrant.

▲ **Eugéne Verdier** (1872). A red member of the group with medium-sized, fragrant, very double flowers.

▲ **Fairy Moss** (1969). The second small-growing moss recently raised by Ralph Moore. Deep pink to light red semi-double flowers appear prolifically.
Général Drouot (1872). The French nurseryman Robert was a prolific producer of roses and this is another of his introductions. Its medium-sized flowers are purple-red and semi-double.

Impératrice Eugénie (1856). A very beautiful moss that blooms profusely and is a tall grower. The flowers are fragrant, medium-sized, double and of a very pleasing lilac-pink.

▲ **James Veitch** (1865). A beautiful variety with deep violet-red flowers that are fragrant, double and of medium size.

▲ **John Cranston**. Not a well known variety. Medium-sized open flowers of light purplish red on a tall-growing plant. Fragrant.
La Neige (1905). Reputedly a sport from 'Blanche Moreau', with more vigorous growth than its parent. It has fragrant, double, white flowers and the foliage turns lovely autumn colours.

▲ **Jenny Lind**. Small, pink, double, fragrant flowers appear profusely on a compact plant which grows to about 1 metre. The buds are strongly mossed.

L'Obscurité (1848). Wine-crimson is the unusual colour of this not so 'obscure' rose. The flowers are loose, semi-double and large.

▲ **Malvina** (1841). Clusters of rosy pink, large, double flowers make this a very attractive hybrid. Vigorous growth, well-mossed buds and good fragrance.

◄**Mme William Paul** (1869). This variety will flower late in the season and has light red, medium-sized flowers. An excellent member of the group that ought to become better known.

▲ **Ma Ponctuée** (1867). A delightful rose which has light red flowers with lighter edges. The medium-sized blooms are plentiful and fragrant on an attractive, compact plant.

Maupertuis (1868). From the French growers, a tall plant which has double, medium-sized flowers of the deepest red. Fragrant.

Mignonne Charmante. A rose that has been common in parts of Europe for a long time. It has pinkish red fragrant flowers of medium size.

Olavus (1932). A more modern addition to the group with medium-sized double flowers that are quite beautiful. Fragrant.

▲ **Mme de la Roche-Lambert** (1851). This variety can produce flowers late in the season. Purplish pink, medium to large flowers with greenish moss. One of the best.

Mme Moreau (1872). A fine variety with large, double, fragrant flowers. They are a rich pink in colour with a white edge to the petals.

▲ Old Black. Although this name is usually applied to 'Nuits de Young', this rose does not appear to have the muddled centre of the former. Perhaps time will tell if they really are different. Small, double flowers, deep maroon-purple and fragrant.

▲ **Paint Brush** (1975). The third of Ralph Moore's small-growing moss roses. Fewer petals than 'Dresden Doll' or 'Fairy Moss', but again flowers are small. Light yellow blooms fade to cream and white.

►**Parkzauber** (1952). A modern variety from Kordes of West Germany. This deep red beautiful rose has a medium to strong scent and medium-sized flowers which adorn a vigorous plant to more than 1 metre.

▲ **Pélisson** (1848). A much-admired rose of yesteryear. Its double, red flowers age to a reddish purple. Fragrant. Grows to a little over 1 metre.

Pucelle de Lille. This distinctive rose has light pink, fragrant flowers and can flower late in the season.

Reine Blanche (1858). A beautiful white variety which has everything going for it. Medium-sized, double, fragrant flowers grow on an upright tallish plant.

Sans Sépales (1839). This variety is distinctive among the members of the moss family because it has no sepals. Double, medium-sized, white and pink flowers.

Sophie de Marsilly (1863). Nice to have another striped moss in the family. A double, medium-sized flower, pink with white stripes. Has a good scent.

▲ **Soupert et Notting** (1874). This rose, with its quite large, pink, very double, scented flowers, was once very popular. A fine variety.

▲ **Souvenir de Pierre Vibert** (1867). An excellent member of the group, sometimes with late blossoms. Dark red and purple medium to large flowers. Scented.

▲ Venus (1904). This not so old variety is bright pink and very double. A medium-sized plant with bright green foliage. Some late bloom.

Violacée (1876). As its name implies, this rose is violet and purple. Nicely scented, double, medium-sized flowers.

Waltraud Nielsen (1932). A more modern member of the family. Pinkish red, lightly scented flowers bloom on a tallish plant.

▲ **Wichmoss** (1911). Until recently, this was the only climbing moss rose. The plant alone is very attractive with its shiny, healthy foliage and heavy moss. The flowers, which appear in clusters, are semi-double, fragrant, small and cream.

◄**Zoë** 'Partout'. Large, light pink, cupped flowers on a tall, branching plant. Distinctive with its very prickly shoots and curiously mossed and curled leaves. A good situation and plenty of attention will reward you with a fine crop of blooms.

Panachée de Lyon

Portlands and their Hybrids

Monsieur Vibert of Angers, whose name seems to be associated with all the early families of roses, once again had a predominant role to play in the establishment of this group. Maybe the early ones came from 'Rose de Trianon' and probably they should be more correctly called damask perpetuals, but, as with some other groups, another name has become the popular title. M. Vibert advised that he had 'formed a new division for an interesting group' and that 'they are desirable and unique in form and colour'.

Some of the old writers enthused about the vigour and fragrance of the group, and in my experience this family certainly does not suffer from a lack of scent. We once left a single flower of 'Yolande d'Aragon' in our large office area overnight, and by the morning the building was saturated with a lingering, haunting fragrance.

The members of this family may well have faults which have turned people away from them, but has not every family faults of some kind or another? In my eyes, they are unsurpassed for form, beauty, colour and fragrance. The theory that this is an unimportant group with little to recommend it is laid to rest by the introduction of another nine varieties here, making a very fine collection of eighteen altogether. ■

Coelina Dubos (1849). A very pretty double pale pink. As with all this family, this attractive rose is recurrent.
►Delambre (1863). An excellent red with medium-sized, double, fragrant flowers. An upright plant, which is the trademark of the family, to about 1 metre.

Jeune Henry (1815). Another red variety which has double, medium to large, fragrant flowers on a tall plant.
Mme Boll (1859). Strongly scented pink flowers make this long-time popular rose still much admired today. It has medium to large double blooms on an upright plant of 1 metre or more.

▲►Marbrée (1858). A large, bright pink rose with white markings. The short-stemmed flowers sit close in to the light green foliage in the manner peculiar to the group.

◄**Marie de Saint Jean** (1869). A very fine white variety which has a strong fragrance. The beautifully shaped flowers are medium-sized and very double, and they nestle very nicely into a plant about 1 metre high.

A Miranda. Of damask origin, this fine variety is bright pink and medium to large, both in the size of the flowers and the height of the plant.

►**Panachée de Lyon** (1895). This rose is sometimes classified as a hybrid perpetual, but it seems to me that it is more at home in this group. Pink, medium-sized, fragrant flowers with purplish red stripes.

Rembrandt (1883). An unusual brick-red colour with white markings which could be called stripes. A tall-growing plant with medium to large double flowers.

Souvenir de la Malmaison Jaune

Bourbons and their Hybrids

History has it that the Frenchman Monsieur Breon found the prototype of this family in a hedgerow on the Isle of Bourbon in 1817. It seems that he grew chance seedlings from this hedge that he then passed on to Monsieur Jacques, the gardener at the Chateau de Neuilly near Paris. According to another story, the bourbon family originated many years before in India, at the Calcutta Botanic Gardens. Your guess is as good as mine as to whether both these roses came from the same source or whether they really were two separate creations.

The introduction of the first bourbons was an exciting time. Hybridists immediately recognised their potential, and their ability to flower twice or more in a season meant a new and wonderful era in rose growing could begin.

The family has china and noisette influences, amongst others, and it is sometimes difficult to place some hybrids in any particular class. According to my research, there appear to be no yellow bourbons or hybrids. (In the last family group described in this book however, you will find some yellow roses that have a bourbon appearance.) There are wonderful whites, pleasing shades of pinks, dark luminous reds and exhilarating striped varieties.

This family is notable for its variations of size and form— there are bourbons that are quite tall climbers, not so tall pillar types, lax shrubs, compact and tall plants and low-growing bushes. ■

►**Acidalie**. A beautiful but little-known rose, as is the next variety also. Its pink-centred white flowers are fragrant and double, and grace a compact plant until quite late in the season.

Adrienne de Cardoville (1845). A typical member of the group with the usual bright green foliage and prominent reddish thorns. The pinkish red double flowers are fragrant and prolific.

Anaïse. Another not so well known rose. Beautiful double, lilac-pink, fragrant flowers.

▲ **Baron Gonella**. Of all the varieties in this group, this one has never failed to impress, and when it becomes better known it should prove very popular. Rounded, cupped, very double, fragrant, bright pink flowers all season long.

Charles Lawson (1853). Built almost in the same mould as the previous rose except that the flowers are larger, the plant is more vigorous, and the colour is a little lighter.

Fulgens (1830) 'Malton'. This hybrid from a china rose was of great importance to the early breeders because it was one of the few fertile bourbons. Bright crimson double flowers.

▲ **Giuletta** (1859). Medium-sized, pinkish white, double, cupped, fragrant flowers on an upright plant of 1 metre or more.

Gros Choux de Hollande. A centifolia hybrid of great beauty, vigorous enough to be a climber. Strongly scented, pale pink, very double, large flowers. An excellent variety.

▲ **Heroïne de Vaucluse**. Another very beautiful member of the group. Deep pink, double, fragrant, cupped flowers on a branching plant.

►**Jean Rameau** (1918). A more recent hybrid which, strangely, is little known. Large, pink, double flowers on a tallish plant.

Mme August Rodriques (1897). Beautiful double flowers of pink and white. Strongly scented and vigorous.

Mme Cornélisson (1865). There is no lack of beautiful roses in this group. This one has very double, lightly scented, white and light pink flowers on a medium-sized plant.

Mme de Sévigné (1874). As with the above variety, little known but beautiful. Large, deep pink and double.

Mme Olympe Teretschenko. Another light-coloured variety of great charm. It too has pinkish white, double, fragrant flowers.

▲ **Mlle Blanche Lafitte** (1851).
An exceptionally pretty rose.
Double, medium-sized and
blush-pink.

Mlle Marie Drivon (1887).
Very double, cupped, fragrant
flowers of bright pink adorn a
tallish, upright plant over a
long flowering season.

▲ **Parkzierde** (1909). Raised by
Peter Lambert, this variety is
an attractive scarlet and deep
crimson. It is very fragrant,
very vigorous and excellent
for cutting.

▲ **Pierre de St Cyr**. An exquisite
member of the group with
profuse, pale pink, cupped
flowers, large and very
double. The plant is very
vigorous.

The Book of Classic Old Roses

►**Prince Napoléon**. My supply
of this beautiful rose came
from Valdemar Petersen of
Denmark. Although little
known, it is a fine variety in
every way. Deep pink,
double, cupped, fragrant
flowers and healthy growth.

▲ **Queen of Bedders** (1878).
Deep magenta-red, semi-
double flowers on a compact
plant. Fragrant.

▲ **Souvenir de la Malmaison
Jaune** (1888) 'Kronprinzessin
Viktoria'. Like its parent, this
rose has very large, flat, very
double, quartered, fragrant
flowers. Differs only in
colour—it is lemon-white with
a deeper lemon shade in the
centre. Very beautiful.
**Souvenir de la Malmaison
Rosé** (1846) 'Leweson Gower'.
This variety, like the former,
shares the features of its
parent in all but colour—this
rose is a deep pink version of
'Souvenir de la Malmaison'.

▲ **Souvenir de Mme Breuil**.
Built in the fashion of 'Mme
Isaac Pereire'. A good grower,
nicely fragrant. Large, very
double, deep cerise- or
magenta-pink.
Venus (1845). Medium pink,
fragrant, double flowers on a
branching plant.
►**Vivid** (1853). To complete this
group, a quite attractive,
bright magenta-red double
flower on a tall-growing
plant.

Morletti

Boursault Roses

Although this group once contained some fifty varieties, they did not achieve great popularity and are now largely lost. It is amazing that five more varieties have come to light for us to enjoy and admire. This is a distinctive group bearing no real resemblance to any other. It seems that in our climate they require a measure of shelter from cold winds and if given the special privileges of food and water they respond in an amazing way. Long canes natural to the group seem to be longer and the flowers along the stems seem to be more prolific and larger under these favoured conditions.

At one time some of the boursaults were used as understocks but they did not prove successful. It was in 1822 that Vibert listed boursaults for the first time and in 1829 Desportes, another French grower, listed four varieties. Vilmorin and Laffay seem to be the only hybridists who had success with the group. It may be that difficulty has been experienced in breeding, and that not many have survived up to this time, but those that have, when they have conditions in their favour, make a glorious and different display, either singly or in groups. ∎

►**Amadis** (1829) 'Crimson Boursault'. A very beautiful rose, although it has no fragrance. The flowers are quite double, rounded and about 10 cm across. They are purple-red and the new growth starts off green and becomes brownish red as it ages.

Blush Boursault 'Calypso'. This member of the group is not as hardy as the others but is nevertheless well worth growing. The quite large, double flowers are blush-pink with much deeper pink centres, and tend to hang on the plant.

▲ **Elegans**. Medium-sized, rosy pink, very double flowers on a healthy plant. Has a long flowering season and an erect, vigorous habit.

Gracilis (1830). Probably a hybrid from *R. arvensis*, from which it gets its vigour and prickles. Flexible growth and prolific semi-double, bright pink flowers.

►**Morletti** (1883) 'Inermis'. Light pink, semi-double, lightly scented flowers. Moderate growth. Has been used as an understock.

L'Ouche

Chinas and their Hybrids

Although representatives of this family did not reach Europe until 1704 at the earliest or 1768 at the latest, there is little doubt that they were known in their native China for thousands of years. It is recorded that in 140 B.C. one of the Han emperors admired a rose, and in about A.D. 1000 nearly fifty different varieties were recognised.

China roses and their hybrids have played a very important part in the establishment of all the families that followed them. Some of the types known to have taken part in the dramatic changes of the period are 'Slater's Crimson', introduced in 1792, 'Parson's Pink' (1793), 'Hume's Blush Tea Scented' (1809) and 'Park's Yellow' (1824). It must be said too, that, although many of the changes were by design, some were apparently unintentional.

Two important facts have emerged from studies of these roses and their hybrids. Firstly, there is a great diversity of appearance among the members of this family and many chinas have ended up being classified in the groups they helped to create. As already mentioned, it takes a brave person to draw the line between groups of roses and a braver person still to place a rose on one side of the line or the other.

Secondly, the colours of most china blooms deepen with age. In recent times we have appreciated this attribute in comparatively modern roses like 'Rumba' (1958) and 'Circus' (1955), but it should be remembered that 'Mutabilis' and others have had this very beautiful characteristic for a very long time. ■

▲ **Arethusa** (1903). A very pretty yellow flower, flushed apricot. Medium-sized, double and prolific on a tidy, compact plant.
Aurore. Another pretty rose with loose, lemon-yellow, double flowers that deepen to salmon-pink. Recurrent.

▲ **Brennus** (1830). A very pretty rose with large flowers of 8 to 10 cm across coloured a rich rosy crimson. They are quite double with wavy petals and appear over a long season.

▲ **Bengale Rouge** (1955). A taller, more recent hybrid which has everything going for it. Bright crimson flowers, large and prolific over a long season.

The Book of Classic Old Roses

▲ **Duke of York** (1894). A very bushy free-flowering member of the group. Small, double, pink and white flowers in profusion.

▲ **Flocon de Neige** (1898). Possibly more at home among the polyanthas but has some china blood in it. Small, starry, white, double and beautiful.

►**Hofgärtner Kalb** (1913). Scented, double flowers, pinkish red with lemon in their centres. Attractive, healthy, vigorous growth.

L'Ouche (1901). A pretty rose with double, rounded, cupped, pink flowers of small to medium size, not unlike a bourbon. Compact, bushy plant to about 1 metre.

▲ Louis XIV (1859). Very deep velvety crimson, small to medium, double flowers which have a dusky look about them. Fragrant and quite beautiful. Compact,

bushy plant.

Mme Eugène Resal (1894). Vigorous growth, and large double flowers that have a yellow base with reddish, orange and pink tinges.

The Book of Classic Old Roses

▲ **Némésis** (1836). A beautiful, small-growing plant with double, purplish crimson, pompon-like flowers. Prolific flowerer on a dwarf plant.

▲ **Papillon** (1882). Not so well known. This very pretty rose is basically pink, shaded white or, at times, deeper colours. Medium-sized, double flowers appear prolifically.

▲ **Pompon de Paris** (1820). A rose with a great history if it all could be known. Some have confused this with other varieties but it stands alone as a fine representative of a bygone era. Double, bright pink flowers in profusion. A dwarf plant, although there is a climbing form of it too.

▲ **Papa Hemeray** (1912). A very pretty rose with single, crimson flowers about 5 cm across with distinctive white areas in their centres. The plant is upright and quite tall.

Princesse Queen. This variety is little known. It is double, white with pink shadings and grows to a medium height.

Rivers' George IV (1820). Believed to be a hybrid from a damask. It has double, cupped, deep crimson flowers which are loose but beautiful. It is fragrant and non-recurrent.

►**Sophie's Perpetual** 'Paul's Dresden China'. A useful rose that has been reintroduced. Deep rose-red with a whitish base. Very fragrant. Compact growth.

▲ **Unermüdliche** (1904). A more recent hybrid which has purple-red and white flowers, medium sized and semi-double. A different, pretty and useful variety.

Bouquet d'Or

Noisettes and their Hybrids

The original varieties of this family, undoubtedly related to *R. chinensis* and *R. moschata*, were reasonably hardy under average conditions, but later members of the group, which leaned towards the tea family, lost some of this hardiness and have therefore survived only in warmer climates, where their beauty remains unsurpassed.

We are all aware of the Empress Josephine's tremendous interest in the development of roses, whether or not her interest was spurred on by rivalry with the Countess of Bougainville. That one lady should contribute so much is history, but that another in a different era should have the opposite effect is not generally known. The story goes that an un-named King of England was well known for his chivalry and the attentions he paid to members of the opposite sex. On one occasion, he went to the gardens in the park outside the palace and gathered a sumptuous bouquet of roses to present to a certain lady at Court. The Queen was absolutely furious when she heard of this latest indiscretion and ordered that all the roses and flowering plants be removed forever from the offending park. If you have the pleasure of walking through Green Park in London today, you will be reminded of this unusual story. You will have to decide for yourself as to the truth of this tale—the details have come to us through popular legend rather than recorded fact, but you have to admit that it could have happened. ■

◄**Autumnalis** (1812). An interesting addition to the family, although there seems to be some confusion about its origins. Double, creamy white, fragrant, medium-sized flowers which are prolific. A fine rose.

Belle Vichysoise (1897). Nice to see this lovely old rose appear again. The flowers are small, pinkish and white, and double. They appear abundantly on a vigorous plant.

Bougainville (1822). Small-flowered, double, bright cerise-pink and quite fragrant. This hybrid is quite vigorous and has a good flush of flower in the spring, followed by a good flowering later.

Bouquet d'Or (1872). A beautiful rose, built in the mould of 'Gloire de Dijon' from which it is a seedling. Very pretty shades of yellow, apricot and copper.

▲ **Capitaine Sisolet** (1885). One of the few red noisette roses to survive. Large, double, fragrant, pinkish-red flowers in abundance. Vigorous growth.

Caroline Marniesse (1848). A beautiful but little-known rose. It is double, creamy white, fragrant and tall growing.

Coquette des Blanches (1871). A variety that has some affinity with the bourbons. Vigorous growth with double, whitish pink, fragrant flowers.

Emilia Plantier (1878). Very pretty shades of yellow, copper and gold. Large, double, quite fragrant flowers. A vigorous and useful variety.

Jacques Amyot. A quite pretty, little-known variety with light pink, medium-sized, double, fragrant flowers appearing prolifically on a tall plant.

La Biche. A very pretty member of the group with double, white flowers that have pinkish edges or shading.

▲ **L'Abundance** (1887). Flesh-pink, smallish, double, fragrant flowers. Not a very vigorous grower but it puts on a brave display.

► **Mme Bérard** (1872). Listed by some authorities as a tea rose. In the style of 'Gloire de Dijon', it has large, double, fragrant, quite beautiful flowers which are apricot-yellow with pinkish tones.

▲ **Mme Driout** (1902). This rose is sometimes classified as a tea or as a climbing noisette. Colour is deep red with large flowers and a nice scent. Strong similarity to 'Gloire de Dijon' in size and shape.

Mlle Marie Gaze (1892). Golden yellow, medium-sized, double, fragrant flowers make this a very beautiful member of the group. Little known.

Marguerite Desrayaux (1906). A beautiful rose with pink shadings. Large flowers which are fragrant and semi-double. Vigorous growth.

▲ **Marie Dermar** (1889). This is a beautiful yellow and white variety with vigorous growth. The double, medium-sized flowers are quite fragrant.

Meteor (1887). A slightly scented, light red variety. Large, double flowers grace a vigorous plant which can have blooms all the way along the arching branches.

Multiflore de Vaumarcus (1875). Deep pink, fragrant flowers, medium sized and quite double. Growth is tall and attractive.

▲ **Nöella Nabonnand** (1901). Another of the group sometimes classified as a tea but equally at home here. Large, semi-double, very fragrant, velvety crimson flowers. Grows to about 3 metres.

Oscar Chauvry (1900). This rose is pink with lemon centres. The colours are nicely combined and the flowers are fragrant, full and medium sized.

► **Reine Marie Henriette** (1878). Tea or noisette?—you can decide. Prolific, nicely scented, bright red, double flowers. Vigorous growth to more than 3 metres.

Reine Olga de Wurtemberg (1881). A regal name for a very fine rose. Quite large, bright red, double flowers. Vigorous growth. A large, very attractive plant when in full bloom.

Roxelane. Pink, double, medium, fragrant flowers on a medium-sized plant. A good variety, little known.

Archiduc Joseph

Teas and Hybrid Teas

When we the present-day enthusiasts look at a family of roses such as this one we should cast our minds back to some of the dedicated men who brought about such wonderful changes in the teas and hybrid teas. It is no fluke that the beautiful colours and forms that we see today owe their origins to men who were looking for that something special. One such rose enthusiast was the French nurseryman, Pernet-Ducher, who was captivated by the stunning brilliance of the flowers of *R. foetida lutea, R. foetida persiana* and *R. foetida bicolor* in the rose gardens in the Parc de la Tête d'Or in Lyon, when he visited that city in the summer of 1885.

His amazement at the deep and beautiful colours present in these roses made him determined to try to introduce them into the roses of the day. Over a long period of time and after many failures he was at last able to produce some seedlings using the pollen from 'Persian Yellow' *R. foetida persiana*.

Remember that when Pernet-Ducher started this programme there were no yellows, bicolours or flame-orange colours present in the garden roses of the time, so when his rose 'Soleil d'Or' was introduced in 1898 a colour revolution had indeed begun. 'Mme Melanie Soupert' and 'Rayon d'Or' followed, and 'Mme Edouard Herriot' were produced in 1913. Because this latter rose won first prize in a contest organised by the London *Daily Mail*, it became affectionately known as the 'Daily Mail Rose'. Pernet-Ducher was at last able to produce a very fine rich yellow in 1920 and he named it 'Souvenir de Claudius Pernet' after his son, who was

killed in the First World War.

The patience and perseverance of Pernet-Ducher in his work with roses is typical of many and I ask you, when next you take time out to admire your particular favourite, to recall the debt we owe to those who have gone before. ∎

Angéle Pernet (1924). An admirable rose that was initially very popular because of its 'new' colour. Large, double flowers of coppery orange, shaded golden yellow. Vigorous healthy growth and a nice scent.

Angels Mateau (1934). Another rose that used to be well sought after because of its colour. It was popular just before and just after World War Two. Strongly fragrant double flowers of orange-salmon, opening in a loose fashion.

Anne Watkins (1962). Quite large well-shaped flowers, usually cream with yellow and pink shadings and with a pale apricot reverse. Double and fragrant, very pretty.

▲ **Antoine Rivoire** (1895). An old favourite with important parents, 'Dr Grill' and 'Lady Mary Fitzwilliam'. Dark foliage contrasts nicely with the cerise flowers, shaded rosy pink. Quite a good scent. Not a big grower.

Archiduc Joseph (1872). A member of that numerous group of beautiful old teas with pinkish red colouring. A strong grower, with shades of orange-pink and deep magenta. A beautiful and unusual rose.

▲ **Atlantis** (1969). Very free-flowering, large, single rose which is 8 to 10 cm across. The colour is an unusual purplish-mauve and the blooms are fragrant.

Augustine Guinoisseau (1889). This is a white colour sport from 'La France' that has inherited all its parent's good points. It is fragrant, large, double and white, sometimes with pink tints.

▲ **Augustine Halem** (1891). May not be correctly named. Quite fragrant, medium-sized, double flowers that appear profusely on a vigorous plant. Coppery pink shades, deeper underneath.

The Book of Classic Old Roses

Barbara Richards (1930). This beautiful variety is basically yellow and buff, with pink reverse. Very large, double, fragrant flowers which droop.

Betty Uprichard (1922). This beautiful rose has upright, healthy growth and fragrant flowers. They are loosely double when open and two-tone, coloured an unusual salmon-pink above and carmine-pink beneath.

►**Black Beauty** (1973). A more recent introduction which one suspects was named to imply being very dark red. Yes, its buds are black-red, but like all of this type they open to a lighter rich scarlet-crimson with a deeper reverse.

Briarcliff (1926). A fragrant, very double, beautiful rose. The flowers have deep pink centres with lighter shades towards the edges of the petals. An excellent rose for indoor culture.

▲ **Catherine Mermet** (1869). Looks rather like the above rose, with well-shaped, large, double, fragrant flowers that have flesh-pink centres, paling towards the edges. Also a good rose for indoor culture.

▲ **Cecil** (1926). A superb single rose with just five petals. The flowers are the deepest possible yellow, about 10 cm across, with stamens almost the same colour.

▲ Colonel Sharman-Crawford (1933). Bright scarlet, double, pointed flowers which are fragrant and velvety. An excellent addition to the red class.

Crimson Glory (1935). A variety that brings back memories to many. Very fragrant, double, well-shaped flowers of deep crimson with purple shadings. A fine climbing form is available as well.

Dame Edith Helen (1926). This vigorous plant has attractive leathery foliage. The extra large, double flowers are bright pink, cupped and fragrant.

Dr Grill (1886). A lovely rose, recently reintroduced after being unavailable for a long time. Very fragrant, nicely shaped, coppery pink flowers.

► Etoile de Hollande (1919). This rose held sway for over thirty years as one of the finest reds and it is still remembered with affection today. Fragrant, double and deep crimson.

The Book of Classic Old Roses

▲ **Golden Dawn** (1929). High-pointed, very fragrant flowers that are deep yellow, paling a little with age and sometimes flushed pink. An old favourite.

Grace Darling (1884). One of the earliest hybrid teas to be introduced. Globular flowers, which are large and double, grace a tall-growing plant. Attractive creamy white, flushed pink.

▲ **Gustav Grünerwald** (1903). A lovely rose from two famous parents 'Mme Caroline Testout' and 'Safrano'. Fragrant, cerise-pink, double, shapely flowers with lemon centres.

Hector Deane (1938). An excellent rose in its day and still sought after. Delightful shades of salmon, cerise and pink, with silver at times. Long stems support nicely shaped buds and the foliage is dark green and glossy.

▲ **Francis Dubreuil** (1894). We are fortunate indeed that this fine rose has survived, and it is good that it seems to be becoming popular once again. Fragrant, nicely double, large flowers of blackish crimson appear profusely.

Freiherr von Marschall (1903). A strong-growing plant which has unusual bright red foliage. Deep carmine-red, double, large, fragrant flowers.

▲ **Homère** (1858). A lovely old-timer. Fragrant, well-shaped, cupped, double flowers of pale pink, shading to white in the centre.

►**Hugo Roller** (1907). The colouring of this rose is exceedingly beautiful. A compact plant with nicely shaped, lemon-yellow, double flowers shaded with rose-red and crimson at the edge of the petals.

Irish Elegance (1905). At one time there were quite a few in this particular group raised by Dicksons of Northern Ireland, and all of them were beautiful and distinctive. Single, about 12 cm across, with five petals. Fragrant, coppery orange and crimson.

Isobel (1916). Another large single rose that excited great comment when first introduced. A light scent and the colour is light pink, with pale apricot centres.

Joanna Hill (1928). A charming rose with large, double flowers, fragrant and creamy yellow with apricot-orange centres. This rose has been used by hybridists in many countries.

▲ **Kathleen Mills** (1934). Large, semi-double, open, fragrant flowers that are pale apricot and pink with a deeper reverse. Healthy plant, upright and spreading.

Lady Alice Stanley (1909). Large flowers on a large plant. Very fragrant, very double, pale pink blooms with a deeper reverse.

Lady Barnby (1930). A lovely silvery pink variety which has well-shaped, fragrant, high-pointed, double flowers. Healthy compact growth.

Lady Mary Fitzwilliam (1882). This rose played an important part in the development of the earliest hybrid teas. Thought to have been lost but has made a welcome reappearance. Large, light pink flowers are very fragrant.

Lady Plymouth (1914). A lovely old tea with long, pointed buds that open out into large, double, fragrant, creamy white flowers.

▲ **Lady Sylvia** (1926). A beautiful colour sport from 'Mme Butterfly'. It differs from its parent in its deep pink flowers, flushed apricot. Long-stemmed and fragrant.

►**Lilac Charm** (1962). Very prolific, large, almost single flowers of lilac-mauve. Fragrant, with golden stamens. Unusual and pretty.

▲ **Lissy Horstmann** (1943). Bright velvety scarlet double flowers sit upright on a healthy plant. A joy to see in full flower.

Lyon Rose (1907). Pernet-Ducher was responsible for this important rose. It has large, double, fragrant flowers. They are pink on the edges and coral pink in the centre, with lemon shadings.

Mme Berkeley (1899). This older variety produces profuse double, fragrant flowers of salmon-pink, cerise-pink and yellow.

Mme Bravy (1846). Beauty is present in all the old teas and this is one of the finest. There are many roses with these shadings but this one stands out. Creamy white with pink tints, double and very fragrant.

▲ **Mme Charles** (1864). This rose came to me from East Germany and does not fit the description generally given. It may be a different rose but is nevertheless beautiful. The buds are deep pink and open lighter pink, paling to blush. Quite small by tea standards.
Mme de Tartas (1859). An important rose long used by hybridists. Lax growth with large, full, scented flowers of blush-pink.
►**Mme de Watteville** (1883). Well-shaped, large, double flowers, lemon with blush-pink edges. Medium growth with a branching habit. Strongly fragrant.

▲ **Mme Edouard Herriot** (1913) 'Daily Mail Rose'. A rose from the Pernet-Ducher stable with quite a history. In 1923 the London *Daily Mail* put forward a prize of £1000 for the best new rose of the year. After much deliberation the prize was awarded to 'Mme Edouard Herriot', even though it had been previously introduced. It became known as the 'Daily Mail Rose' and enjoyed great publicity over a long period. Even today it is still being asked for by that name. Its parents are unknown. Its colouring was new to the family and, like several others in this group, it has been used extensively as a parent by breeders in search of fresh colours.

The plant has large red thorns on the young growth and an upright habit. The flowers are a little more than semi-double, large and quite fragrant. The colour is difficult to describe but contains shades of coppery orange, old rose-pink and lemon-yellow. We certainly have a lot to thank Pernet-Ducher for.

Mme Elisa de Vilmorin (1864). This is one of the earliest members of the family. It has upright, tidy growth and quite large, double, deep carmine flowers which are very attractive.

▲ **Mme Jules Gravereaux** (1901). This is a tall grower, often classified as a climber. Distinctive flesh-pink colour shaded deeper pink and lemon. Good fragrance. Healthy foliage and growth.

Mme Louise Laperriere (1951). Attractive, very fragrant, double, scarlet flowers. A more recent introduction, but somehow looks older, possibly because it comes from 'Crimson Glory'.

▲ **Maman Cochet** (1893). A fine rose from two excellent parents, 'Mme Lombard' and 'Marie van Houtte'. Flowers have pale pink edges with deep centres and lemon throats. Large fragrant blooms and dark foliage.

Mrs Edward Laxton (1935). Old rose and salmon, large, double flowers on a healthy plant. At one time a very popular rose.

Mrs Foley Hobbs (1910). A delightful rose of robust habit. It has double, fragrant, creamy white flowers at first then white with pale pink edges.

Mrs Sam McGredy (1928). At one time a very popular rose in both bush and climbing form. Its colour has not really been reproduced in any other rose. The flowers are pointed in the bud and open to coppery orange and pink with deeper reverse. Branching habit.

▲ **Mrs Wemyss Quin** (1914). One of the earliest yellow tea roses. The double flowers are a deep yellow with orange-shaded outer petals when fresh. The flowers are fragrant and high-pointed in the bud.

▲ **Monsieur Tillier**. Quite large, very double flowers. Reddish buds open to almost carnation-like blooms of deep pinkish salmon that then pale to pinkish shades. A strong, healthy plant with reddish young growth.

Perle des Jardins (1874). An excellent rose for indoor culture. Very fragrant, globular, straw-yellow flowers produced prolifically on a plant of slender growth.

Princesse de Sagan (1887). An unusual rose with medium-sized purplish-shaded buds opening to purplish crimson flowers with crinkled petals. Medium growth and fragrant.

►**Shot Silk** (1924). After all these years this rose is just as popular as ever, with its cherry-pink double flowers, its strong fragrance and its healthy growth and foliage.

▲ Souvenir d'Elise Vardon (1885). A little-known member of the group. Fragrant, double, bronzy yellow flowers with cream tones. Very pretty.

Souvenir de Mme Léonie Viennot (1898). A tall-growing variety that can be trained as a climber. The flowers are double, large, yellow and bronze, and may be quartered.

Souvenir de Pierre Notting (1902). An attractive rose, coloured yellow, pale apricot and bronze. The blooms are very double, long-pointed and fragrant.

The Book of Classic Old Roses

Souvenir de Thérèse Levet (1886). A useful older member of the family. Double, fragrant, light red flowers in profusion.

Souvenir du Président Carnot (1894). Another rose from that inimitable French breeder Pernet-Ducher. Scented, pinkish white, large, very double flowers on a medium-sized, upright plant.

The Bride (1885). A sport from the beautiful 'Catherine Mermet', differing from its parent only in colour—it is white with a pink blush.

►**Triomphe du Luxembourg** (1840). Coppery salmon and pinkish buff double flowers which are strongly scented. A fine, very old rose.

Vesuvius (1923). Of relatively recent origin with modern colouring. Large, almost single, six-petalled flowers are deep velvety crimson with golden stamens. Luxuriant foliage and growth.

▼ **Violinista Costa** (1936). Deep pink, shading nearly to red. Glossy healthy foliage and upright growth.

▲ **White Wings** (1947). The last in this group but probably one of the most beautiful. Large and single and the purest white. Fragrant with distinctive chocolate anthers.

Eclair

Hybrid Perpetuals and their Hybrids

This family is famous firstly for the very large number of varieties it contains and secondly for the continuous debate surrounding the inclusion of many of those varieties into this classification.

The French grower and hybridist, Laffay, is usually credited with the creation of the first roses of this group as early as 1837 and it is amazing that so many of them have survived to the present day. That they have done so is in part because of the establishment of the rose gardens at Sangerhausen in the German Democratic Republic. The idea of creating this wonderful collection of roses was conceived by Peter Lambert in 1897, becoming a reality in 1903. Today it must be one of the oldest and largest collections of roses anywhere in the world.

The gardens are on a hillside overlooking the very old and beautiful town of Sangerhausen and although one may require a certain amount of tact and patience to get there, it really is worth the effort. From the moment you step off the train and walk across the cobblestone square, there is an air of ancient expectancy abroad. You travel through streets paved with slabs and cobbles and lined with beautiful old two- and three-storeyed sharp-roofed houses amidst very old trees, until you reach the magnificent wrought-iron gates of the gardens. You are then taken on a journey through history as you read the names of the roses, so many famous people and places commemorated by the beautiful blooms. You will never forget the sheer joy of being present and being able to observe the rare, distinctive fragrant roses on that hillside site overlooking the town, which may not realise the

priceless treasure it has at its doorstep.

A huge man-made mountain, a copper mine I believe, stands nearby and seems to act as a silent sentinel for all to know that the magnificent rosarium is close at hand. ■

Anna de Diesbach (1858). This may be a seedling from 'La Reine' and it certainly shares some of that beautiful rose's features. Tall growing to 2 metres with double, large, fragrant flowers. They are cupped and deep rose-pink with deeper pink in the centre.

▲ **Captain Hayward** (1893). A useful addition to the family. It has light red flowers which lighten towards the edges. Double, fragrant and large-sized blooms are followed by largish orange fruit.

Charles Gater (1893). A strong-growing plant that has attractive, large, very double flowers of bright red. They are fragrant and appear not to purple with age.

Charles Lefèbvre (1862). Strongly scented and very double, this tall-growing variety has cupped flowers of reddish crimson which become purplish red as they age.

▲ **Comtesse Cécile de Chabrilliant** (1858). A beautiful rose. Medium-sized, deep rose-pink flowers, with a strong fragrance, bloom profusely on a strong, healthy plant.

▲ **Duke of Edinburgh** (1868). An upright, tall, attractive plant which has medium-sized, double, fragrant flowers. They are scarlet-crimson and make a fine sight at the peak of the season.

▲ **Duke of Wellington** (1864). A very free-flowering member of the group that would be attractive in any company. It has a very strong scent and the flowers are reddish crimson and velvety. They are large and double and bloom on a tall-growing plant.

The Book of Classic Old Roses

▲ **Dupuy Jamain** (1868).
Magenta-red is the colour of
the attractive, double, fragrant
flowers of this variety. The
growth is upright, healthy and
profuse.
Eclair (1883). An unusual
combination, for this group, of
a vigorous plant and small,
double flowers. Very double,
well-shaped and blackish red
with deeper shadings. Nice
scent.
►**Elisa Boelle** (1869). A strongly
fragrant, vigorous-growing
rose of interesting beauty.
Cupped blooms with petals
that incurve. The flowers are
large and pink with a deep
pink flush.

▲ **Empereur du Maroc** (1858).
Every now and then a
different rose appears in a
group. This member is quite
distinctive with its small, very
double, purplish crimson
flowers. They are fragrant
and profuse. The plant is

short and compact.
Enfant de France (1860). Very
double, large flowers of silvery
pink appear on a tall plant.
They are fragrant and the
petals have a velvety texture.
An excellent rose.
Erinnerung an Brod (1886)

'Souvenir de Brod'. Although
this is a *R. setigera* hybrid it
can be grouped with the
hybrid perpetuals. A fine rose
with quartered flowers that
are very double and fragrant.
They are cerise-pink, crimson
and purple.

The Book of Classic Old Roses

Ferdinand de Lesseps (1869) 'Exposition de Brie'. Nicely shaped flowers on a vigorous plant. They are quite double, fragrant and a pleasing shade of cerise-purple.

Fisher Holmes (1865). An excellent member of the group with healthy foliage and attractive flowers which appear prolifically. They are scarlet and deep crimson, large and double. Quite fragrant.

Géant des Batailles (1846). This older variety is generally considered to be one of the favourites of the family. Very double, blood-red, fragrant flowers.

 George Dickson (1912). Large intense crimson flowers that have a lingering fragrance. Much sought after at one time for potpourri, and gaining popularity again today. Healthy plant with the best flowers appearing on lateral growths.

▲ **Gloire de Bruxelles** (1889). This member of the group is large in every way, with very robust growth, very large flowers and a very strong scent. Purplish crimson in colour.

▲ **Gloire de Chédane-Guinoisseau** (1907). Similar in some ways to the previous rose. Large flowers, very double, on a strong-growing plant. Cupped, fragrant flowers of reddish crimson.

►**Gloire Lyonnaise** (1885). The product of two very fine roses, 'Baroness Rothschild' and 'Mme Falcot'. The flowers are large, semi-double, fragrant and pure white, yellowing at the base. A tall-growing, healthy plant.

▲ Heinrich Schultheis (1882). Another variety that is large in every way. The soft pink blooms are very large, very double and very fragrant, appearing on a vigorous plant.

Her Majesty (1885). Very large, rose-pink, double flowers with a good fragrance. The beautiful blooms may have cerise-pink in their centres.

►Horace Vernet (1866). Crimson-red, large, double, high-pointed flowers, strongly fragrant. Compact, upright growth.

Jean Rosenkrantz (1864). Not a very well known variety, but quite pretty and useful. Upright, healthy growth supports large flowers of reddish pink. Medium scent.

Jean Soupert (1875). Deep purple-red blooms, large, full and fragrant, adorn an upright, healthy plant.

Marguerite Guillard (1915).
Apparently a sport from 'Frau
Karl Druschki'. Semi-double
flowers open flat and white.
Prominent yellow stamens.
Merveille de Lyon (1882).
This variety is a sport from
'Baroness Rothschild'. An
exceedingly beautiful rose,
blush-pink and white.

▲ **John Hopper** (1862). Another
member of the group which is
large in every way. Globular,
very double flowers which are
bright pink with mauve edges
and darker centres. Very
fragrant.

Le Havre (1871). A pretty rose
with attractive leathery foliage
on a compact plant. Dusky,
brickish red double flowers.

▲ **Oskar Cordel** (1897). Has the
previous rose as one of its
parents. Not a large grower,
but has extremely attractive
blooms which are an even
carmine-pink. They are
fragrant, cupped and appear
profusely.
Paul's Early Blush (1893) 'Mrs
Harkness'. Reputedly a sport
from 'Heinrich Schultheis'
which it resembles in many
ways. Pale pink, large, very
double, fragrant, beautiful
flowers.
Pierre Notting (1863). An
upright, tall-growing variety
that is notable for its rounded,
double flowers, deep crimson,
with darker shadings.
Fragrant.

▲ **Jules Margottin** (1853).
A variety that has been used
extensively as a parent. Large,
double, deep cerise-pink
flowers which open flat.
Fragrant.

▲ **Mme Scipion Cochet** (1872).
Strong-growing, very double,
medium to large flowers. They
are purplish pink in the centre
paling towards the edges.
Petals curiously wrinkled.

▲ **Ruhm von Steinfurth** (1920). Another large-flowered member of the family with huge, deep crimson-red blooms, very double and strongly scented.

▲ **Souvenir d'Alphonse Lavallée** (1884). A very lovely member of the group with shadings of purple and crimson. On looking at this rose one can see similarities to many other good red roses. Strong fragrance.

►**Souvenir de Jeanne Balandreau** (1899). An unusual colour for a member of this group. Well-shaped, large flowers of deep pink, flushed with orange-pink. They are medium sized, double, and nicely fragrant.

Souvenir de la Reine d'Angleterre (1855). A very strong grower that can put on an excellent late flowering. It has large, double, bright rose-pink, fragrant flowers and is reputed to be a seedling from 'La Reine'.

Triomphe de l'Exposition (1855). An excellent member of the family with bright red and purplish crimson double flowers that are large and well scented. This rose is sometimes confused with several others.

Victor Hugo (1884). Attractive magenta-red and purplish crimson flowers, medium sized, double, rounded and quite fragrant. They appear profusely on a vigorous plant.

Amélie Gravereaux

Rugosas and their Hybrids

Although the popularity of these roses was very slow in coming there is little doubt that they are held in very high regard today, prized for their tremendous hardiness and their ability to produce plentiful, fertile seed. They have a special beauty and charm that stand them apart from any other family.

Their tremendous hardiness sees them being naturalised in areas where most other roses would not stand a chance, such as coastal regions (for example, both the eastern and western seaboards of the United States), railway embankments and motorway edges in the United Kingdom, many parts of Western Europe, Siberia, Manchuria and extensive areas of coastal and inland Japan.

We know of the excellent work done by the early hybridists such as Bruant, Paul and Cochet-Cochet, and the more recent work by Valdemar Petersen of Denmark who has created some beautiful rugosa hybrids. However, not much is known of the beautiful hybrids raised by Seizo Susuki in Japan. It seems fitting that a man from the home of the original rugosas should have been instrumental in creating several lovely varieties, so different from those already known. Hopefully these will become available to everyone in due course.

Two new forms, one red, one white, of the well known, low-growing 'Max Graf' are included in this selection, beautiful recent hybrids from the very old established rose-growing house of Kordes in West Germany. ■

Amélie Gravereaux (1900). A strong-growing member which, like most of the family, is very prickly. The flowers are medium-sized, double and very strongly scented. Deep purple-red with the beautiful foliage typical of the group. Recurrent.

▲ **Atropurpurea** (1899). The combination of *R. rugosa* with *R. damascena* produced this very pretty hybrid. It is single, fragrant, medium sized and coloured an attractive carmine-crimson.

▲ **Culverbrae** (1973). This recent hybrid has large, very double, very fragrant, crimson flowers. A fine display of bloom at mid summer is followed by an intermittent display.

▲ **Caporosso.** A more recent hybrid with bright scarlet, double, fragrant flowers which have a flush of orange. The foliage and growth of the plant is typical of the family.

▲ Dart's Dash. Purple-red, double, medium-sized flowers set amidst bright green foliage. Large, orange fruit late in the season. Not very well known but quite useful.

Dr Selma Lagerloef. Large orange-red fruit typical of the group grace a leafy plant of about 1 metre. The flowers are double, pink and quite different from others in the group.

Fürstin von Pless (1911). A hybrid from 'Mme Caroline Testout' and 'Conrad Ferdinand Meyer' which could be placed here or in the tea family. A pretty rose with white and pink fragrant blooms on a tall-growing plant.

Golden King (1935). A sport from 'Dr Eckener', this rose is quite different to the preceding one. Very fragrant, semi-double, loose flowers, pale yellow and recurrent.

Goldener Traum (1932) 'Golden Dream'. An excellent, relatively recent variety with pure deep yellow flowers and pinkish red streaks on the buds. Large, very fragrant blooms and the plant is healthy and vigorous.

Mme Ancelot (1901). Large, double flowers, white flushed pink, on a tall-growing plant. Good scent.

►Mary Manners (1976). A recent addition to the family that is well worth having. Purest white, double flowers appear prolifically on a tall plant. Well scented.

▲ **New Century** (1900). A hybrid that should be better known. Nicely scented, large, double flowers of deep pink with centres that darken to red.

▼ **Rote Max Graf** (1980) 'Red Max Graf'. Although this is a very recent introduction from the West German nursery of Kordes, it is built in the same mould as the original 'Max Graf'. Large, almost single, crimson flowers with lemon centres. Lightly scented.

Rugosa Copper (1955). This relatively recent hybrid is a colour break from earlier ones, as recent hybrids so often are. Large, bronzy orange flowers appear profusely on a vigorous plant.

Sanguinaire (1933). Remarks for the previous rose apply to this one too. The colour jolts you out of any rugosa sameness you may have imagined. Bright blood-red with orange shades and prominent yellow stamens. The flowers are loosely semi-double, lightly scented and large.

►**Signe Relander** (1928). Small-flowered and semi-double, a medium grower with a noticeable fragrance. The colour is a bright deep red and the blooms are produced freely. Not unlike the 'Grootendorst' group.

Typica. A name not accepted in some circles today but still in use. Some species have been grown from seed and others have been collected from many different places and this of course leads to many variations. Large, single, cerise-pink and fragrant.

Sir Thomas Lipton (1900). A tall-growing hybrid that could be used as a climber. The flowers are double, nicely cupped and sweetly fragrant. They are white, sometimes flushed pink and form a good contrast with the deep green foliage.

Trollhättan. It is a pity that this beautiful rose is not better known. Double, lilac-pink, fragrant flowers appear profusely on a medium-sized plant.

Vanguard (1932). An unusual hybrid which has won several awards. Tall, growing to 3 metres or more. It has fragrant, double, salmon-apricot flowers. Probably inherits its very shiny foliage from *R. wichuraiana*.

▲ **Variegata**. Purple-red single flowers. Foliage has distinctive variegation or striping of pink and yellow.
Weisse Max Graf (1983) 'White Max Graf'. Like 'Red Max Graf', a very recent hybrid from Kordes in West

Germany, similar to its parent. Pure white flowers with lemon centres, nicely scented. Glossy, healthy foliage.
White Hedge. A beautiful, single, white variety that has attractive large fruit in late summer and autumn.

Bloomfield Dainty

Hybrid Musks and Varieties

Having presented an excellent group of these very fine roses previously one would have thought that it was not possible to do that very same thing again. But this is not the case and we have before us again an interesting group of hybrid musks.

I sometimes wonder if Peter Lambert, the German nursery-man, realised the importance of his rose 'Trier' in the development of the beautiful hybrid musk family. I recently had the privilege of visiting the city of that name, and when standing outside Lambert's Garden Centre, it occurred to me that no one really knows at the time it occurs that some particular happening will have a far-reaching future effect. Not only has Peter Lambert's rose 'Trier' been the foundation stone of this family, but Lambert himself was a man of great foresight who was instrumental in the creation and development of the famous collection of roses at Sangerhausen.

Ingomar Lang, director of Sangerhausen

Trier is a most beautiful city, nestling on a river flat, in the bends of the river Moselle and on the hills and valleys nearby. Created by the Romans and nurtured by other peoples over its 2000 years of history, it is no wonder that Lambert, a native son of this city which holds the preservation of everything old so dear, should have been responsible for the preservation of old roses on a grand scale at Sangerhausen.

There seems to be no end of pretty hybrid musks and I believe the following group maintains the standard set in my first volume, *The Book of Old Roses*, in terms of colour, shape and type. ■

Aurora (1923). An excellent variety created by the Rev. Joseph Pemberton, who did so much for the development of this family. Small, semi-double flowers, medium yellow fading to creamy white. Quite fragrant.

Ausonius (1932). Reasonably tall-growing plant with rather pretty coloured flowers, reddish yellow when in bud and pinkish yellow when open. The plant flowers profusely and the blooms are fragrant and semi-double.

Bloomfield Dainty (1924). An exceptionally pretty rose of at least three colours: bronzy apricot buds become bright yellow flowers that fade to cream or off-white. The single flowers, 5 cm across, appear in clusters and are fragrant.

Callisto (1920). Another Pemberton production. Small, yellow, double flowers in groups sit upright on a medium- to tall-growing plant.

▲ **Ceres** (1914). A fragrant variety that has semi-double, pale pink flowers with lemon tints, enhanced by bright yellow stamens. Profuse blooms on a medium-sized plant.

▲ **Charmi**. It is a pity that this member of the group is so little known. Pretty pink double flowers in profusion. Fragrant.

Clytemnestra (1915). An award-winning Pemberton hybrid. Fragrant, small, double flowers on a spreading, healthy plant. The bronze buds open to a dusky salmon. Flowers all season.

▲ **Daphne** (1913). Deep pink, small, semi-double flowers, strongly scented. Attractive tall-growing plant.

▲ **Erfurt** (1939). A useful, more recent addition to the family. The flowers are large, semi-double, rosy carmine near the edges and lemon towards the centres. Fragrant and long flowering.

Fortuna (1927). Sometimes listed as a hybrid tea. A beautiful rose with semi-double, large, rose-pink, fragrant flowers.

Gartendirektor Otto Linne (1934). An attractive variety with deep cerise-pink flowers with white centres. Petal edges deepen with age. Profuse double flowers adorn a vigorous plant.

Heinrich Conrad Söth (1919). Small single flowers of pink with white centres appear over a long period on a vigorous plant. Scented.

Hoffman von Fallersleben (1917). A lovely rose created by Peter Lambert. Small, double, pinkish red flowers with yellow shadings appear prolifically on a tall-growing plant.

Inspektor Blohm (1942). Very double, strongly scented, medium-sized, white flowers. The flowers contrast very nicely with the greyish green foliage of the vigorous branching plant.

▲ **Maid Marion** (1930). Another of the numerous hybrids bred by Pemberton. Beautiful, large, semi-double, white flowers in profusion.

►**Marie-Jeanne** (1913). Nicely scented, medium-sized, double, white flowers, sometimes with blush shadings. Forms a compact plant to about 1 metre, and is quite thornless.

Morgensonne (1954). Another beautiful rose from the house of Kordes. Very large, fragrant, golden yellow flowers, cerise-pink in the early opening stages. Good growth on a healthy vigorous plant.

▲ **Mozart** (1937). A bright cheerful member of the group — might have guessed it came from Lambert. Small, single, cerise-pink flowers with prominent white centres appear in large clusters on a healthy plant.

►**Pink Prosperity** (1931). A rather pretty, blush-pink, rosette-type flower in clusters. Nicely scented and quite vigorous.

▲ **Queen of the Musk** (1913). Strongly scented, small, double flowers that appear profusely on a tall-growing plant. The blush-white blooms open from quite dark buds.

Rivers' Musk (1925). Another Pemberton introduction. Small-flowered, double, pinkish red and strongly fragrant.

Rostock (1937). Flowers very large and double, light pink and fragrant. Prolific blooming season. Attractive foliage dark and shining.

Sangerhausen (1938). Another beautiful hybrid from Kordes. Large, cupped, semi-double, light red flowers on a large plant with healthy foliage and growth.

Surf Rider (1968). Although quite recent, this hybrid is cast in the mould of most of the family. Very free-flowering, fragrant, double and creamy white.

Violet Hood (1976). Small, pompon-shaped, deep violet flowers on a strong-growing plant. Strong fragrance. An unusual colour and a welcome addition to the group.

Blaze Superior

Shrub-climbers and their Relatives

Included in this family are varieties that are sometimes referred to as pillar roses, which may have added a little to the confusion about the members of this group. Pillar roses could be defined as slow-growing climbers attaining a height of about two metres, which, when tied to pillars or other supports, develop into very beautiful plants with flowers well distributed over a long flowering period. They can also be grown free-standing by encouraging side growth instead of upright growth.

This selection includes some reasonably modern varieties as well as quite old ones, and there are several more *R. eglanteria* hybrids, making a good group of them overall. There are two more members of the 'Frühlings' family raised by Wilhelm Kordes, making a total of eight in that subgroup.

When researching the source of so many roses and rose families, one cannot but be amazed at the number raised and introduced by the Kordes' establishment in West Germany. 'W. Kordesöhne' is now in its third generation, proceeding with excellent work in the hybridising field, producing both modern roses and varieties with an older look. This famous and well-respected business has created hundreds of roses over a long period of time and we the growers, collectors and enthusiasts are so lucky to have been able to have access to these wonderful creations. We are also very fortunate that a grandson of the founder Wilhelm, also named Wilhelm, is continuing with the work in a most gracious and conscientious way. ■

▲ **Aïcha** (1966). Valdemar Petersen of Denmark raised this beautiful rose. The flowers are large — 12 cm or more — semi-double and very fragrant. They are deep yellow and the plant and blooms bear quite a resemblance to 'Frühlingsgold'.

▲ **Angelina** (1976). A very pretty rose, recently introduced. Flowers about 8 cm across are bright cerise-pink at the edges, paling to white or lemon-white in the centres. Fragrant and free flowering.

▲ **Ash Wednesday** (1955) 'Aschermittwoch'. An unusual and pretty rose. The buds are greyish white and the large, quite double flowers open to a light greyish brown fading to dull white. Strong grower, flowers profusely.

Autumn Fire (1961). A lax-growing plant to about 2 metres which has abundant blooms. The flowers are deep red with deeper shadings and they are followed by a heavy crop of large orange-red fruit.

Ayrshire Queen (1835). An old but important rose which is deep purplish crimson and semi-double. It is said that the mark of this subgroup is vigour and hardiness although this member is not quite so strong growing.

Ayrshire Splendens 'Myrrh-scented Rose'. Tall, growing to more than 4 metres. Said to be a hybrid from *R. arvensis*, inheriting its long trailing shoots. Fat red buds open to double, cupped flowers of medium size. They are creamy white and deliciously fragrant.

Baltimore Belle (1843). Profuse flowering late in the season only, and as it is a hybrid from *R. setigera*, this is understandable. Drooping clusters of double, flesh-pink, cupped flowers.

Blaze Superior (1950). Very similar to 'Paul's Scarlet', but able to produce a later crop of flowers. Grows to about 3 metres and has a light scent.

▲ **Copenhagen** (1964). An excellent hybrid from the Poulsen stable. Very large, double, deep crimson flowers over a long period, nicely fragrant. Foliage is bronzy when young.

Frank Naylor (1978). If you are looking for something different then this could be the rose. An upright shrub with single, scarlet-crimson flowers with lighter centres. Fragrant.

▲ **Break o' Day** (1939). An unusual rose with shades of orange and pink and a strong fragrance. The double flowers are large and profuse.

▲ **Fairyland** (1980). Of a spreading rather than a climbing habit and therefore very useful for ground cover. Small, double, rose-pink blooms, lightly fragrant, appear in clusters. Glossy, healthy foliage.

Flammentanz (1955). A useful modern addition to the family, although it is non-recurrent. Large, fragrant, crimson-scarlet flowers in profusion and attractive dark foliage. Grows to 3 metres.

▲ **Fred Loads** (1968). One of the brightest roses about today, never fails to impress. Large, 10-cm, semi-double flowers are bright orange paling to much lighter centres. Strong growing to about 2 metres.

▲ **Frühlingschnee** (1954) 'Spring Snow'. Very large, semi-double, purest white, lightly fragrant flowers. Upright tall growth.

Frühlingstag (1949) 'Spring Day'. Very fragrant, large, semi-double, golden yellow flowers that appear profusely in one flowering. Grows to 2 metres.

Frühlingstunde (1942) 'Spring Hour'. Medium, semi-double, lightly scented flowers that are white with a pink flush. The plant grows to about 2 metres and like the other members of this subgroup is quite prickly.

►**Greenmantle** (1895). Flowers are single and bright pinkish red with a white eye. A hybrid from *R. eglanteria* with the typical fragrant foliage. Vigorous.

▲ **Hamburger Phoenix** (1954).
An excellent rose from Kordes.
Large, loose flowers of rich
velvety crimson-red. Repeat
blooming and vigorous
growth.
Hanseat (1961). Lightly
scented, single rose-pink
flowers, medium sized and
cupped, appear upright on a
tall plant.
Hein Mück (1961). This and
the previous hybrid were both
raised by M. Tantau of West
Germany in the same year.
Bright red, medium-sized,
single, cupped flowers.
Hermann Löns (1931).
Luminous, light red, large,
single flowers on a vigorous
plant to 2 metres or more.
Quite a good scent. Glossy,
healthy foliage.
Ilse Kröhn Superior (1964).
Nicely shaped, pointed,
double flowers that are cream
at first deep down, changing
to pure white. Strongly
fragrant. Grows to about 2
metres.

▲ **Janet's Pride** (1892)
'Clementine'. Said to be a
hybrid between *R. damascena*
and *R. eglanteria* that was
found by chance. Very pretty,
semi-double, small flowers,
rosy red towards the edges
and white in the centres.
Julia Mannering (1895). Tall
growing with fragrant foliage.
Small, single, pale pink
flowers in profusion. Nice
scent.

▲ **Kassel** (1956). A fine recent
introduction from Kordes.
Loosely double, orange-scarlet
flowers appear over a long
period. Grows to 3 metres.
La Belle Distinguée 'Scarlet
Sweet-Brier'. A hybrid with
the fragrant foliage typical of
the subgroup. Small, very
double, bright crimson
flowers, non-recurrent.
Lichterloh (1955). Velvety,
blood-red, semi-double, lightly
fragrant, medium-sized
flowers on a vigorous plant.

▲ **Lichtköengin Lucia** (1966). Deep yellow, medium-sized, semi-double flowers on an upright plant to 2 metres. Medium fragrance.

▲ **Lord Penzance** (1894). Sweetly scented foliage, as with other members of the group. The bright red hips are preceded by single, coppery yellow flowers with pinkish tints.

▲ **Lykkefund** (1930). A very attractive thornless rose that has one profuse flowering in mid summer. The blooms are small and just semi-double, creamy yellow fading to white. Strongly fragrant and very vigorous.

▲ **Mannheim** (1959). Recurrent flowering on a plant to 2 metres. The flowers are large, double and crimson and they appear in large clusters.

▼ **Manning's Blush** (1832). Quite pink buds open to small, double, blush-pink flowers that pale to white. Fragrant foliage.

The Book of Classic Old Roses

▲ **Plentiful** (1961). A very
beautiful rose from Le Grice.
It has large, double flowers of
deepish pink built in the old
style. They are abundant on a
healthy plant.

▲ **Morgengrüss** (1962). Very
double flowers have unusually
coloured petals with cerise
and rose-pink edges, a flush
of yellow, and cream centres.
A pretty variety.

▲ **München** (1940). Medium-
sized, semi-double, scarlet-
crimson flowers with yellow
centres. Lightly scented.
Vigorous growth and prolific
blooming.

▲ **Pearl Drift**. One of the many
beautiful roses produced by
Edward Le Grice. It is one of
the few hybrids from

'Mermaid' and that other
popular rose, 'New Dawn'.
Double flowers, white flushed
pink, appear over a long season.

Rote Flamme (1967). Deep blood-red, medium-sized flowers that are double and profuse. Tall-growing, very hardy plant.

►**Scintillation** (1968). A lax-growing shrub that can be grown as a large bush or made to climb. It has large clusters of very fragrant, semi-double, blush-pink flowers.

▼ **Soldier Boy** (1953). A very bright single climber. Profuse, bright scarlet, five-petalled, large flowers with deep yellow stamens.

Pride of Hurst

Polyanthas and their Relatives

It is with great pleasure that I am able to present a much larger group of polyantha roses than in my first volume, *The Book of Old Roses*. The following selection includes a number of varieties from some of the world's leading hybridists and it is a great delight to have at last been able to find and make available 'Paquerette', the rose considered to be the first polyantha.

These beautiful and interesting roses should never be allowed to disappear, and that they have survived is in many ways miraculous. They have grown quietly, often in secluded places, cherished by dedicated rose-lovers and exhibiting their deceptive beauty for the unwary to be captured forever. For over 100 years most of them have held a secret, which no doubt was the source of their inner strength; that one day their true worth would be recognised. Little did we know that this worth would stand out in the 1980s when all over the world people have, for various reasons, taken up residence in dwellings with very small gardens. There is therefore a new demand for showy roses that do not grow too tall, such as the members of this beautiful family. We have an exciting time before us, to appreciate those polyanthas that we thought were lost and to learn to admire and enjoy those which are actually new and yet have that miraculous oldness about them. ■

▲ **Britannia** (1929). Large clusters of small, single, crimson flowers with white centres appear recurrently on a compact plant. Light green leaves nicely set off the dark flowers.

▲ **Cameo** (1932). One of the members of this group that has remained consistently popular because of its pink colouring. The small flowers are cupped, salmon-pink and appear in clusters. Lightly fragrant.

►**Dainty Maid** (1940). This beautiful single rose which flowers in clusters probably should be classified as a hybrid polyantha but fits in well in this group. The colour is silvery pink with cerise reverse.

Dick Koster (1929). As with many of the hybrids in this family this rose originated as a colour sport from another, then in its turn created other varieties in the same way. Deep pink flowers in trusses.

▲ **Doris Ryker** (1942). A very pretty shade of salmon-pink. The medium-sized flowers appear in clusters and are fragrant. Bound to be popular when better known.

Ellen Poulsen (1911). Bright cherry-pink, large, double, fragrant flowers in large clusters. Dark, shiny foliage and bushy growth. Recurrent flowering.

Fireglow (1929). Dwarf compact growth. Small, very bright orange flowers, single and lightly scented, appear in clusters.

The Book of Classic Old Roses

▲ **Gloire du Midi** (1932). Brilliant orange and scarlet flowers are small, rounded, double and lightly fragrant. Growth is bushy and the foliage light green and leathery.

Gloria Mundi (1929). Very bright orange-red, small, double flowers in clusters. Light green, glossy foliage. One of the features of most of these polyantha roses is their habit of colour sporting. This hybrid, a sport itself, is no exception.

Ideal (1921). The dark, shiny foliage of this variety blends very nicely with its deep velvety crimson, rounded, open flowers. Lightly scented.

Jean Mermoz (1937). A very strong-growing hybrid that has small, very double, deep pink flowers. They are unusual in that they are imbricated or lacinated. Lightly fragrant.

►**Katharina Zeimet** (1901). A fine rose from Peter Lambert. Small, white, double flowers in clusters. Medium scent. Grows into a compact, bushy plant.

Lady Reading (1921). This is a sport from Ellen Poulsen that has small, rounded, bright scarlet flowers in clusters. Dark green foliage and dwarf growth.

▲ **Leonie Lamesch** (1899). A variety that because of its colour was really ahead of its time. The semi-double flowers have yellow centres and bronzy red or deeper red edges.

▲ **Marie Pavié** (1888). Semi-double flowers, 5 cm across, form loose, upright clusters. Blush-pink buds open to pretty, flesh-white blooms. Nice scent.

Maywonder (1968). This recent introduction is a blood-red sport of 'Muttertag' ('Mother's Day'). Growing to only about 35 cm high, it makes a fine pot or edging plant.

Muttertag (1950) 'Mother's Day'. Grows to about the same height as the above hybrid. The colour is deep red, and the blooms are double, clustered and prolific.

▲ **Margot Koster** (1931). An excellent rose for a small hedge or edging. Salmon-coloured flowers are small, rounded and fragrant and appear in small, tight clusters.

▲ **Mrs R. M. Finch** (1923). Rosy pink, double flowers that pale with age. They are medium sized, profuse and appear in clusters.

▲ **Nypel's Perfection** (1930). Large, semi-double, bright pink flowers shaded a deeper pink appear in clusters on a healthy, vigorous plant.

▲ **Orléans Rose** (1909). Semi-double, bright rosy red, small flowers with white centres. As with all the group, flowers appear in clusters. Light scent. Flowers late in the season.

Paquerette (1875). Recognised as the first of the polyantha class and worth growing for this if no other reason. Small, double, white flowers in large clusters. Compact growth.

Paul Crampel (1930). Attractive, light green foliage offsets the deep orange-vermilion blooms that appear in large clusters.

▲ **Pride of Hurst** (1926). A very pretty colour sport of 'Coral Cluster' that is very popular today. Very double, small, rosette-type flowers are salmon-pink fading to blush and white.

Renoncule (1913). Small, double, rounded flowers in clusters are deep rose-pink with lighter shadings. Upright compact growth and a little scent.

►**Sheelagh Baird** (1934). Large clusters of large, quite double, light pink flowers. They are deep rose-pink towards the edges and have a lemon base. Strong grower.

▲ **Sneprincesse** (1946). This variety grows to little more than 30 cm, so it is often used as a pot plant, especially in Europe. Pure white double flowers.

►**Vatertag** (1959) 'Father's Day'. An orange-scarlet sport of 'Mother's Day' that grows to about 35 cm, the same height as its parent. Suitable for pot plants or edging.

Woody. Not so well known. Dark carmine-red flowers of medium size appear in clusters on a compact plant.

Francis E. Lester

Climbers and their Hybrids

As if we were not already fortunate enough in being able to appreciate all the bush forms of roses, nature has blessed us with an extension of this same beauty in every climbing rose. Bush forms are often actually enhanced by being in climbing form — for example, when a rose has the habit of hanging its head or, to put it another way, is weak in the neck, this feature is turned to advantage in the climbing form where one looks up at the blooms rather than down on them.

The beauty of climbers is appreciated throughout the world. In mid California, climbers can be seen adorning an old building, such as a tea-house or gazebo, or decorating very large arches and wooden trellises in the Huntingdon Botanic Gardens.

Many beautiful climbers can be found in the magnificent grounds of Hampton Palace Court gardens, outside of London, and in the Royal Horticulture Society gardens at Wisley and the Botanic Gardens at Kew.

The Tivoli gardens in Copenhagen and the Palace gardens in the city of Trier in West Germany beautifully display climbing roses, and all down one side of the Tokyo Municipal Rose Gardens is a marvellous display of both old and more modern varieties, trained as pillar roses on poles. It is a joy to walk the length of this very effective row of climbers.

The following selection includes many beautiful climbers, from a number of families and with a wide range of parents. We may not be able to define the complex sources of the climbers described hereafter or classify them precisely, but we do understand the beauty they bring to all parts of our world. ∎

▲ **Adam** (1833). A very old tea rose which at one time was thought to have been lost forever. Nicely scented, semi-double, large flowers of medium pink.

▲ **Allen Chandler** (1923). A vigorous grower that produces large, almost single flowers of bright crimson with prominent golden stamens. Also has a prolific crop of large orange-red fruit when encouraged.

Ards Pillar (1903). Large, double, deep velvety crimson, fragrant, healthy blooms. This rose and the following one were both raised by A. Dickson of Northern Ireland.

▲ **Ards Rover** (1898). An old beauty that is available again. Sometimes recurrent, it has large, double, crimson flowers, nicely shaped and fragrant.

▲ **Chaplins Pink Climber** (1928). A hybrid from two famous parents, 'American Pillar' and 'Paul's Scarlet Climber'. It is very vigorous and very free flowering in one season and has large, semi-double, bright rose-pink flowers with yellow stamens.

The Book of Classic Old Roses

▲ **Château de Clos Vougeot** (1908). Of sprawling habit and medium growth. The many-petalled flowers are deep velvety red with darker shades and open flat with golden stamens showing. Very fragrant.

Crimson Glory (1946). Very fragrant, deep velvety crimson flowers are large, double, cupped, vigorous and prolific. The bush form was introduced in 1935 and the climber 11 years later.

▲ **Dainty Bess** (1935). A climbing form of the very beautiful bush variety. Similar in every way to the bush with its large, single, soft pink flowers and darker stamens.

Etoile de Hollande (1931). Very free-flowering, bright red blooms are cupped, double and very fragrant. An excellent variety that seems to have stood the test of time.

▲ **Francis E. Lester** (1946). A very pretty rose which is not as popular as it should be. The flowers are single, about 5 cm across, white with pink edges, and appear in large clusters.

Guinée (1938). Another dark beauty rarely seen these days. It has large, double, fragrant, blackish crimson flowers.

Mme Edouard Herriot (1921). The climbing form of the so-called 'Daily Mail Rose'. It is coral-red with yellow shadings and opens to loose, semi-double flowers. Vigorous.

Mme Pierre S. du Pont (1933). Excellent, deep golden yellow, double, fragrant flowers sit upright on a vigorous plant.

▲ **Mary Wallace** (1924). An extremely pretty sight when in full bloom with flowers all the way along the arching branches. The colour is a bright rose-pink and the flowers are large, semi-double and fragrant.

Meg (1954). An extremely beautiful rose. Large, almost single flowers are pink with a flush of apricot and have dark stamens. Fragrant. Grows to about 3 metres.

Mrs Sam McGredy (1938). This climbing form has very special appeal with coppery salmon-pink double flowers in profusion over a long season. It is fragrant and has quite dark young foliage.

Ophelia (1920). Another treasure from yesteryear. Double, beautifully shaped, flesh-pink flowers with deeper shadings and lemon centres. Very fragrant.

▲ **Paul Lédé** (1913). It seems that there is no end of beautiful roses in this group. Apricot-pink, large, nicely shaped flowers. Strong scent.

Paul's Lemon Pillar (1915). With parents like 'Marechal Niel' and 'Frau Karl Druschki', this hybrid could not fail to be beautiful. Very large, strongly scented, pale lemon blooms. They are not recurrent.

Paul's Himalayan Musk. An extremely vigorously growing hybrid which has dainty sprays of pale lilac-pink flowers with a very sweet scent.

Réveil Dijonnais (1931). Even if this hybrid never flowered it would make a very attractive plant with its beautiful dark green foliage. Bright orange and red flowers with yellow centres. Semi-double and lightly scented.

Richmond (1912). Medium-sized, double, cerise and bright scarlet flowers are freely produced and nicely scented. Grows to about 4 metres.

Sénateur Amic (1924). Large, almost single flowers of the brightest carmine-pink. Vigorous growth and heavy perfume.

Shot Silk (1931). After all the years since its introduction this hybrid still excites admiration from many people. Very shiny foliage on a very upright and strong-growing plant. Bright cerise-pink flowers shading to lemon in the centres. Very fragrant.

Souvenir de Mme Léonie Viennot (1898). This old hybrid seems to have everything. Recurrent flowering, strong tea scent, vigorous growth to 5 metres and healthy foliage. Dark buds open to deep yellow flowers with bronze and copper shadings.

Vicomtesse Pierre de Fou (1923). Strongly scented and very vigorous. The flowers are large, double, bronze-orange and pink. They are very fragrant, often quartered and quilled, and are produced as profusely in autumn as in mid summer.

Souvenir de Claudius Denoyel (1920). Very large, double, scarlet and crimson flowers with deeper shadings.

Fragrant. Profuse flowers in mid summer with some later blooms. An excellent red climber.

Aglaia

Ramblers and their Relatives

It seems that the number of rambling varieties that have survived is almost endless — there are almost 100 varieties listed in this and my first volume, *The Book of Old Roses*, and there are more out there.

One outstanding feature of this family is the wonderful range of colours it contains. Scarlets, crimsons and light reds are predominant, and the pinks range from one end of the spectrum to the other. Whites and near whites are plentiful, and the more unusual bluish, purple and grey shades are well represented in this family. There are oranges and apricots, and although there is really no deep yellow as we know it today, there are several which come, at least in the early stages, very close to it. And then there are the indefinable colours which border on all these.

As well as a marvellous range of colour, ramblers also have great diversity of form: from simple, five-petalled flowers to those with many petals, from reasonably double to extremely double, and from blooms of 3 cm across to those 10 or 12 cm in diameter. Some have little or no scent, but the majority are medium to strongly fragrant.

And so we have at hand a marvellous group of roses that are very adaptable and endurable, giving you pleasure in every conceivable way, and, although we enjoy these present members of the family, we wait with bated breath and more than a little enthusiasm for the modern hybridists to turn their attentions in this direction. ■

Aglaia (1896). The first of the three ramblers named for the Three Graces. Intensely fragrant. Recognised as the first light yellow rambler.

Semi-double, lemon-yellow flowers fade to whitish lemon.

▲ **Alida Lovett** (1905). A very beautiful light pink with lemon at the base of the petals. The flowers are large and double and nicely fragrant. Mostly flowers only once over a long period.
Améthyste (1911). The fifth rambler in this colour group. Violet and crimson flowers, quite small and very double, appear in large trusses. Vigorous growth and flowers are non-recurrent.
Apple Blossom (1932). One of the few roses raised by Luther Burbank. A superb hybrid with pink flowers that have lighter centres and wavy petals. Vigorous growth.

▲ **Aristide Briand** (1928). An unusual but very pretty member of the family. Fragrant double flowers are mauvish pink at first, paling to light mauve-pink and white. The blooms are in large clusters and the foliage is shiny and healthy.
Astra Desmond. A little-known rose with small, double, white flowers in clusters. Strong growing with a light scent.

▲ **Auguste Gervais** (1918). Extremely fragrant and vigorous, reaching 6 metres or more in height or in length. The large blooms are salmon-pink within and bronzy reddish pink without, and are nicely contrasted with the dark foliage.

▲ **Bobbie James** (1961). A latecomer to the group, but beautiful and worthwhile in every way. Vigorous to 6 or more metres. Very fragrant, medium-sized, semi-double, creamy white flowers with prominent golden stamens.
Breeze Hill (1926). Large flowers, very double and cupped, are rose-pink and lemon-buff. Vigorous growth, strongly fragrant.
Buttercup (1909). A hybrid of great beauty and rarity. It has small yellow flowers, not quite single, that appear in clusters. The plant is vigorous and has light green foliage.

The Book of Classic Old Roses

Coupe d'Or (1930). Medium-sized, double, deep yellow in its early stages, paling later. Fragrant. A healthy plant with shiny foliage and profuse fragrant flowering.

Crimson Conquest (1931). Not unlike 'Bloomfield Courage' but with larger single crimson flowers. Blooms are profuse and fragrant and appear in large clusters on a strong-growing plant.

Crimson Rambler (1894) 'Turner's Crimson Rambler'. An important rose which had a great influence on early rose breeding. It has large clusters of double, small, crimson flowers which purple with age.

Dawson (1888). A vigorous-growing rambler that produces clusters of small, double, bright pink flowers. Nicely fragrant.

▲ **Euphrosyne** (1895). The second rose named after the Three Graces. The flowers are quite small, very double, rounded and fragrant. They appear in clusters and are rich pink at first, fading to pink and finally pale pink.

▲ **Flora** (1855). Sweetly scented, double, lilac-pink flowers, with darker centres. Has one abundant flowering period. Dark-coloured foliage and strong, healthy growth.

▲ **Dorcas** (1922). If for nothing else, this rose will be remembered as the parent of 'Achievement', the rose with variegated foliage. It has very pretty, salmon-pink, rounded, small flowers in clusters.

Dundee Rambler. Very strong-growing with huge canes and large thorns. Has the ability to grow in shady places. Small, double, white flowers, tinged pink.

▲ **Evangeline** (1906). Pretty, single, fragrant pink flowers, about 5 cm across, appear in clusters. Quite a good late season. Tall growing to 4 metres or more.

François Foucard (1900). An excellent hybrid raised by the French nurseryman Barbier, who pioneered work with rambling roses in Europe. Semi-double, medium-sized, lemon-yellow flowers in clusters. Vigorous plant and shiny foliage.

François Guillot (1907). From Barbier again. Lightly fragrant, medium-sized, double flowers on a vigorous plant. The colour is white with a lemon flush.

François Poisson (1902). Another Barbier hybrid. A vigorous grower with large, double, pale yellow flowers, sometimes with apricot centres. Flowers pale with age.

Général Testard (1918). Not very well known. A tall-growing variety with small, white-centred, semi-double, crimson flowers.

Jean Guichard (1906). Another fine rambler raised by Barbier. Flowers are a lovely shade of coppery pink with crimson buds and attractive foliage. Strong growing.

La Perle (1904). One of the largest growing ramblers, reaching 8 or 9 metres. Very strong scent and double blooms of creamy white with darker centres. A fine rose.

Lime Kiln. This attractive hybrid is well-known in Western Europe. It has small, quite double flowers in profusion that are pure white when open and lemonish in the bud.

Lyon Rambler (1909). An excellent member of the group. It is strong growing with medium-sized, semi-double blooms of carmine and bright pink.

Madeleine Selzer (1926). Sometimes referred to as 'Yellow Tausendschön'. Strong growing with few thorns. The flowers are pale lemon fading to white and they are scented.

▲ **Mme Alice Garnier** (1906). This is a very beautiful rambler and we are indeed fortunate to have access to it. Dainty foliage that is always shining and beautiful, different, I think, to any other. The flowers are about 5 cm across and of a soft salmon-pink with quilled petals. Extremely fragrant.

Maria Lisa (1936). A non-recurrent hybrid with small, single, pink blooms with white eyes and abundant yellow stamens.

Marie Gouchault (1927). An early-flowering variety which is very strong growing. It has small, double flowers, bright red paling to pink, in large clusters.

Marietta Silva Taroucová (1925). Deep green foliage and very vigorous growth. Large, bright rose-pink flowers in profuse clusters.

Paul Noël (1913). Large flowers, up to 8 cm across, semi-double, pink and lemon in colour. A strong grower.

▲ **Paul Transon** (1900). A beautiful hybrid from Barbier. A free-flowering plant with glossy foliage and large, strongly scented salmon flowers, bronzy in the bud. Grows to about 5 metres.

◄**Primevère** (1929) 'Primrose'. Rather modern looking with large flowers that are deep yellow in the bud, opening to a medium yellow. Blooms sit nicely in clusters on a plant that has rich green shiny foliage. Light scent.

Purple East (1900). Unusually coloured reddish purple, medium-sized, almost single flowers appear early in the season. Attractive, glossy, light green foliage.

▲ Rambling Rector. A very vigorous and very fragrant rambler which has the ability to climb up and over trees, hedges and buildings. Semi-double white flowers with yellow stamens.

►Seagull (1907). Can be described in a similar way to the previous one, but its flowers are single, about 3-4 cm across, and have golden stamens. It is becoming very popular.

Shower of Gold (1910). This excellent hybrid used to be popular between the two world wars, and it is nice to see that it is available again. It is a very vigorous grower and has double, rosette-like flowers of golden yellow which pale later to lemon-yellow.

Snowflake (1922). Not to be confused with the tea rose of the same name. This hybrid has very fragrant, double, white flowers in clusters on a vigorous plant.

▲ **Spectabilis** (before 1848). This sweetly scented rose is daintiness personified. Fully double perfect rosettes of rose-pink which soon turn to creamy white. An important and excellent rose.

▲ **Thalia** (1895). An excellent white which is a hybrid between 'Paquerette' and *R. multiflora*. Small, double, white, very fragrant blooms in large clusters. Vigorous growth.

This hybrid is the third of the group raised by M. Schmitt of Lyon, France, and named after the Three Graces who were goddesses of ancient Greece. Apparently these three, Aglaia, Euphrosyne and Thalia, were the personification of light, joy and fertility and the inspirers of the arts, the sciences and all graceful activities. It has taken me some time to collect all three hybrids and they are indeed beautiful. Some writers have suggested that they have lost their charm but I have not found this to be so and have them planted in a group where passers-by can see them and enjoy their grace, gentleness and beauty.

▲ **Thelma** (1927). Profuse, large, semi-double flowers are bright pink with darker shadings. Lightly scented and almost thornless. Grows to about 3 metres.
►**Thiona**. A very pretty hybrid which has bright green healthy foliage on a strong-growing plant. The deep gold buds open to small, semi-double, deep yellow flowers paling to lemon. The three colours together have a nice effect within the clusters.

▲ **White Flight** (1923). Light green foliage and a tall-growing healthy plant. Semi-double medium-sized flowers that are pure white and appear in large trusses.
White Tausendschön (1913). A colour sport from 'Tausendschön' that has inherited all of its parent's attributes. The foliage is a lighter green than the parent's and sometimes the flowers have some pink coming through.

Ellen

English Roses

This is an additional classification to the first volume, that has become necessary because of the foresight and courage of one man who was astute enough to realise that new old-looking roses could be created by using one old parent and one modern one. David Austin of Albrighton near Wolverhampton is just that man, and it could be said that he is ahead of his time because he is the pioneer of this kind of hybridisation programme. Others have worked along these lines, but none has carried out the extensive work over something like twenty-five years that David Austin has accomplished. He has had an ideal shining as a beacon in front of him — the wish to create old-looking roses with more modern colours and the ability to flower again.

David Austin

I can vouch for his success, having grown a number of his introductions here in my nursery and having seen most of the rest of them in his nursery in England. 'Constance Spry' could be said to be the beginning of his vision and since its introduction in 1961 up until the Chelsea Show of 1984, about fifty varieties have been created in the Albrighton nursery. David Austin must now be a very happy man.

I am certain that these roses will stand the test of time. There are some that form compact, low-growing plants and some that grow taller. The colours are a joy to behold. Pale apricot, deep yellow and the deepest possible crimson are among the new colours. Most are fragrant and all but three flower more than once in a season. And, as if all that is not enough, they look like beautiful old gallicas, damasks, albas, bourbons and species.

I have no doubt that these 'new' old roses will be well received as they become better known and we must consider ourselves very fortunate to have access to them. ∎

▲ **Admired Miranda** (1982). This strongly fragrant hybrid has blush-pink rosettes which are fully double. They sit upright on a hybrid tea type bush which grows to about 1 metre. **Belle Story** (1984). Very large, semi-double blooms which, when open, are flattish and incurved with prominent golden stamens. They are silvery pink, strongly scented and produced freely on a plant to about 1.5 metres. **Bredon** (1984). This recent hybrid has small, double, buff-yellow rosettes. The small-growing plant quickly produces wood from the base which helps maintain a succession of flowers.

▲ **Canterbury** (1969). This beautiful hybrid is one of David Austin's earliest introductions. The flowers are 12 cm or more across and loosely semi-double. The petals are wavy, the colour is bright rich pink paling in the centre and the fragrance is heavy.

Most of the early roses produced in this group were named for the works of Geoffrey Chaucer. One can be forgiven for allowing one's mind to wander back in history while viewing such roses as 'Canterbury', 'Wife of Bath', 'The Knight' and others, as the raiser pays tribute to those characters of yesteryear. Is it too fanciful to suggest that roses like these ones were known in those days?

▲ **Charles Austin** (1973). Grows to about 1.5 metres. The strongly fragrant blooms are cupped, quite double, very large and have shadings of apricot and yellow, and pale with age.

▲ **Charmian** (1982). This hybrid has large, flat, very fragrant flowers that are double and will quarter at times. The colour is bright rose-pink and the plant grows to about 1 metre.

▲ **Chaucer** (1970). An excellent rose for smaller gardens. Strong fragrance of myrrh. The flowers are medium, double, rose-pink and profuse on an upright compact plant.

▲ **Chianti** (1965). This beautiful non-recurrent hybrid has large, crimson, double flowers that purple with age. They are gallica-like and very fragrant. Large healthy plant to 1.5 metres.

▲ **Cressida** (1983). Again a hybrid with a strong myrrh scent. Vigorous-growing plant to nearly 2 metres. The flowers are apricot-pink, double and medium sized.

▲ **Cymbaline** (1982). Light greyish pink is the unusual colour of this hybrid. The blooms are saucer shaped, double and fragrant. The arching branches have flowers in profusion and the plant is healthy, growing to more than a metre.

▲ **Dame Prudence** (1969). The medium-sized flowers are double and very fragrant. They open flat and are soft pink with a lighter reverse. Prolific flowering.

▲ **Dapple Dawn** (1983). A sport from 'Red Coat'. This member of the group has large, single flowers of blush-pink. It is in bloom constantly on a plant of 2 metres.

▲ **Graham Thomas** (1983). An excellent rose that marks the work that Graham Thomas has done to popularise old roses. It has medium-sized, cupped flowers of rich deep yellow that are nicely fragrant. They are bourbon-like in appearance, and bloom freely on a healthy plant, to about 1.5 metres.

On a recent visit to the United Kingdom, I was instructed to visit Castle Howard in Yorkshire, not only because of the collection of roses there but also to meet the very knowledgeable man in charge of the grounds, Jim Russell. Before leaving New Zealand I cherished the hope that I might be lucky enough to meet and talk to Graham Thomas, the doyen of old rose enthusiasts. Upon arriving at Castle Howard, my wildest dreams came true when who should be visiting that day but Graham Thomas himself.

The three of us spent all afternoon and most of the evening together and afterwards I realised how fortunate I had been in meeting these two gentlemen — on the one hand to be present when two men of such great knowledge were together, and on the other to be able to take part in their exhaustive discussions on plants and trees of all kinds. It is fitting that such a beautiful rose has been named after Graham Thomas and my cup of happiness was overflowing when I parted from them both, late that night.

▲ **Dove** (1984). Small, double flowers of blush-white begin as blush-pink buds, and appear in dainty sprays on a spreading plant. Lightly fragrant.

▲ **Ellen** (1984). Large, fully double flowers which are cupped and strongly fragrant. They are a soft apricot darkening towards the middle, and the edges pale with age. A robust plant of more than 1 metre.

▲ **Fair Bianca** (1982). A beautiful rose, creamy white on opening, that becomes pure white. The flowers are medium-sized, reminiscent of a damask and have a good fragrance. Height 1 metre.

▲ **Glastonbury** (1974). This hybrid has a heavy damask fragrance. The rather beautiful blooms are large with curled petals. They are deep crimson, later becoming dusky purple, and show golden stamens.

▲ **Heritage** (1984). A very beautiful rose truly built in the mould of the old ones. Its flowers are medium sized, cupped and quartered. They are blush-pink and exquisitely fragrant. Repeat flowering.

▲ **Hero** (1982). Not unlike the bourbon 'La Reine Victoria'. Large, double, cupped flowers of pure pink in the first flowering, sometimes semi-double in the second. Richly fragrant. Height more than 1 metre.

Hilda Murrell (1984). Named after an old-rose pioneer. This rose has large, flat flowers of deep bright pink which are powerfully fragrant. Considered to be one of the finest of these English roses.

Immortal Juno (1983). Powerfully fragrant, large, double, glowing pink flowers open flat and appear freely on a strong, healthy plant.

Jaquenetta (1983). A particularly free-flowering hybrid which puts on an excellent display. The flowers are large, single, soft pink and pale apricot. Sometimes they appear singly and sometimes in clusters.

▲ **Leander** (1982). Small, very double flowers which appear in large clusters, deepish apricot and quite unique in their petal formation. A very beautiful rose with a strong scent.

▲ **Lilian Austin** (1973). A little more modern in its looks than most of the group. Lovely arching habit and the blooms appear freely over a long period. They are fragrant, salmon-pink with orange and apricot shadings, and semi-double with wavy petals.

Lordly Oberon (1982). Deeply cupped, large, fragrant flowers of delicate pink. The plant grows to over 1 metre high and produces these truly old-type flowers freely.

▲ Pretty Jessica (1983). An ideal rose for the small garden, growing to about 1 metre. It is a warm rich pink with a strong fragrance. The free-flowering blooms are double and cupped.

▲ Lucetta (1983). The semi-double blooms are at least 10 cm across and can appear singly or in twos or threes on an arching plant. The colour is blush-pink fading to white.

Mary Webb (1984). The paeony-like flowers are pale yellow and quite large. They are fragrant and sit well on a strong-growing shrub.

Moonbeam (1983). This hybrid has a few more petals than a true single and it has a very good profusion of flowers. Glowing white and fragrant.

▲ Prospero (1982). Although not the easiest rose to grow, the effort is worth it. The rich, deepest possible crimson flowers are gallica-like in appearance, forming neat rosettes.

▲ Mary Rose (1983). Named to mark the recovery of Henry VIII's flagship. A beautiful rose with a damask fragrance that seems to be always in flower. Rich pink double flowers adorn a healthy twiggy plant which grows to over 1 metre.

▲ Perdita (1983). This hybrid is typical of the effect achieved by this group. The flower looks old, being flat across the top, quite double, medium to large and sometimes quartered. But the colour, blush-apricot, is modern. Sweetly fragrant.

▲ Proud Titania (1982). Again, the old with the modern. A damask-like flower, medium sized, fragrant and pure white but with a modern flush of pale apricot at times. Reaches about 1 metre.

▲ **Red Coat** (1973). Crimson-scarlet, large, single flowers are produced in profusion on a bushy healthy plant to about 1.5 metres. An excellent rose for mass planting because of its continuous flowering.

▲ **Shropshire Lass** (1968). This is a vigorous grower to over 2 metres. The non-recurrent flowers are large, flat, almost single and flesh-pink. Lightly scented.

▲ **Sir Clough** (1983). One of the brightest members of the group, coloured a bright deep pink with contrasting stamens. It is a lusty grower and the flowers are semi-double and freely produced.

▲ **Tamora** (1983). This is a paeony-like rose with pretty apricot colouring. Strongly scented, large, double, cupped flowers on an upright plant growing to 1 metre.

▲ **The Friar** (1969). Medium-sized, semi-double, very fragrant flowers, freely produced. They are blush-pink at first, paling to white, and contrast with the dark green foliage.

▲ **The Knight** (1969). A free-flowering variety with excellent growth and deep green foliage. The colour is the deepest crimson with purple shades later and the medium-sized, very double, very fragrant flowers open flat.

▲ **The Miller** (1970). Tall growing to more than 2 metres and very hardy. It has double, cupped, fragrant flowers of the clearest possible pink.

▲ **The Reeve** (1979). Globular, quite double, dusky pink flowers in profusion on a spreading, arching plant which grows to about 1.5 metres. It has a strong, old-rose fragrance.

►**The Squire** (1977). A very beautiful hybrid with large, flat flowers with many petals, and golden stamens that just show. The blooms are an unfading crimson and they have a rich fragrance.

▲ **The Prioress** (1969). This hybrid has light green foliage and is vigorous with upright growth. It is nicely fragrant, blush-pink and cup-shaped with the stamens showing.

The Book of Classic Old Roses

▲ **The Yeoman** (1969). A very useful smaller-growing hybrid with salmon-pink, medium-sized flowers which open flat and are very fragrant. The healthy plant flowers very freely.

▲ **Wenlock** (1984). Lush, deep green foliage sets off the crimson, double flowers very well. Blooms are flat and strongly perfumed. Repeat flowering.

►**Wife of Bath** (1969). Another of the group well suited to the smaller garden. A tough, reliable rose which bears charming rose-pink blooms with a strong scent. Mostly in flower.

▲ **Troilus** (1983). Unusual honey-buff large flowers, which are double and cupped, grace a medium-growing plant. They have a sweet scent, are freely produced and repeat well.

▲ Windrush (1984). This hybrid is not unlike 'Golden Wings' but has a much longer flowering season. The pale green foliage is graced by almost single flowers of lemon-yellow with prominent stamens and a strong fragrance.

Wise Portia (1982). This richly fragrant hybrid is unusual because of its purple flowers. The blooms are fully double and quite exquisite in their form. Not a vigorous grower.

▲ Yellow Button (1975). A delightful little rose with small, short-petalled rosettes in small clusters, yellow with deeper centres. Shiny, healthy foliage and a nice fragrance.

►Yellow Charles Austin (1981). A sport of 'Charles Austin' with lemon-yellow flowers. Like its parent, it has large, cupped blooms with a strong scent.

PART THREE

Propagation and Identification

'Beauty is truth, truth beauty,' — that is all
Ye know on earth, and all ye need to know.

Keats

Propagation and Identification

There is such a great wealth of information about roses and their history that no one man can ever hope to put it all together. It is a very vast and complex subject and there are times when I have felt that these two volumes have done little more than scratch the surface. This year will be my forty-second budding season. Yet sometimes when I feel like straightening my back for a while, having just completed a group of buds and ties, I stand upright between the rows to gaze over the garden and feel that after all these years I really do not know anything about roses at all. It is my firm belief that there really are no experts. There is no one with all the answers. Of course, there are people with knowledge, and some with more than others, but I would like to remind readers of Alexander Pope's words:

> A little learning is a dang'rous thing;
> Drink deep, or taste not the Pierian spring;
> There shallow draughts intoxicate the brain;
> And drinking largely sobers us again.

I am quite certain that there is a growing future for old roses in all their forms. It is not necessary to once again list their many attributes or to wax lyrical about their form and fragrance. Their worth is being recognised by a growing number of people all over the world. Folk from all walks of life have experienced their charm and usefulness, and although it has been a slow awakening, there is no chance that the interest will be allowed to sleep again. Reflecting this growing interest, our display garden in Temuka is continually developing. As the years go by, each family has more members added to it so that the collection now numbers over 1200 in total. These have come from many countries and are available for all to see and enjoy, and it is our desire and pleasure to propagate and distribute them.

PROPAGATION

The methods of propagation used by growers everywhere are always a subject of interest and discussion. As a result of more than forty years of rose and plant propagation, I had formed certain opinions about methods of increase and it was gratifying to have my ideas confirmed by my recent travels to California, the United Kingdom, Western Europe and Japan. It seems that growers the world over are satisfied that the best way to increase roses is to bud them in the summer season or graft them on to a root-stock in the winter season. The root-stocks used in the different countries are *R. laxa*, *R. inermis*, *R. canina* var. *R. multiflora* and 'Dr Huey'. Without going into the pros and cons of propagation, it is fair to say that rose growers everywhere would

◄*A glasshouse at Arowhenua featuring the standard 'Nozomi' (1968)*

not use this method, with all its inbuilt difficulties, unless it was the best available.

When you are dealing with nature you are working with some intangible power that, when it so desires, can wipe mere man aside, as if he was a fly on a whale's tail. Have you ever stopped for a moment and thought about the fierceness of the sea when it is angry; how strong the whipping wind can be; how destructive and unbearable fire is when it is on the rampage; how powerful rivers are when they are in flood and how hot the sun's rays can sometimes be? We the growers and producers of roses are left stranded at times by those same forces. We cannot prevent the frost, or the hail, or the wind, nor control the sun or the rain or the lack of them, and although we might know how to do the right thing at the right time, it is not always easy or possible to do so.

This is particularly evident during the three months of summer, the budding season of the year. The root-stocks are in the best possible condition for budding when they have grown a little, still with plenty of room to move easily. If we work on them too early, the sap will not yet be running freely and yet if we leave them until too late in the season, when their growth is mostly over, the bark will not lift as it did and they are really not worth working on.

Similarly, precise timing is necessary when working with the budwood. Early-cut budwood can be immature and only a small percentage of it will grow; budwood cut at the optimum moment will give excellent results; and budwood cut late in the season can be too stringy or the buds may have shot into growth too much and it is really too late to try them. Obviously, the budding process is a complex one, but it must be said that when everything goes according to plan it is also a most satisfying one.

Some roses can of course be grown from cuttings. During my travels, I visited two well known international rose gardens where many of the established plants had originally been grown in this way. However, there was no comparison between the roses in these gardens and those elsewhere that had been budded or grafted. I am sorry to say that the branches were thin and spindly, there were too many of them, the overall growth was short, the foliage was correspondingly smaller and weaker and, most important of all, the flowers were smaller, shorter and lacked vitality. As a result of all this, the life of the plant would probably be shorter also.

As a result of my research and my years of experience, I am more than ever convinced that roses do better in every way when they are budded on to a root-stock. Experiments by many overseas growers have shown that although a few roses thrive happily on their own roots, most, when grown from cuttings, do not flourish to the same extent as those on another root system. Even roses successfully increased by tissue culture seem unable to carry their early promise on into later life.

IDENTIFICATION

Already touched on in Part One of this volume, I feel that more needs to be said on this matter to those who keep on asking for the names of their old favourites. Since World War II, many hundreds of rose varieties have passed through the hands of rose growers everywhere. If you look through a rose list of say thirty years ago, you will find very few names that you can recognise and very few of them will be available today. No matter how large or small a nurseryman's or grower's establishment may be, each year he is faced with having to decide which varieties are to be kept for another year and which are losing vitality or popularity and should be discarded to create room for new varieties. Over the last forty years I have seen something like 1200 varieties of roses discarded, and every other grower has probably experienced the same. So, when you arrive on the premises of your nurseryman or supplier with a rose plucked from the front garden of the property you have just purchased, and you know that the

plant has been there for at least thirty years, you really have not got much chance of finding its true name, unless it happens to be one of the very few to survive from that period.

Recently we had a lady bring us two roses to identify and I tried very hard to explain to her that the chances of being able to identify flowers from a bygone era were slight and I spent a considerable amount of time explaining the reasons why, as written here. It seemed impossible to make her understand and I allowed myself an inward smile when she started her car and said through the open window, 'Huh, you really do not know much, do you?'

The flower in fact plays the smallest part in the identification process — perhaps twenty-five percent compared to seventy-five percent that I would allow for the rest of the plant — its growth, hardiness and everything else that pertains to its existence. I cannot emphasise the complexity of the identification process enough. Be the roses ancient or modern, the chances of a positive identification are remote. Some seasons ago I decided that no matter where a rose came from we would not accept its name as correct until time or circumstances proved its identity. I do not think that anyone sends out wrongly named roses intentionally, but it does happen and it takes some time to discover the mistake and more time to correct it.

Paul's Himalayan Musk

ROSE GROWERS

In the course of my work and since completing the first volume of *The Book of Old Roses*, many people from all over the world have inquired where they can purchase rose plants. The following short list contains the names, addresses and telephone numbers of some of my fellow old-rose growers. They are people with whom I have made contact over the years, having had the privilege of exchanging both varieties and visits with most of them. These growers carry a large number of different varieties and may be able to procure others if your demand for a particular rose is great enough. Because the U.S. Agriculture Department does not allow imports of rose material from New Zealand, I would remind keen rose collectors from that country that Denmark has most of what you would like and if not it can be sent to them from New Zealand.

My two growing contacts in Australia are Deane and Maureen Ross of:

Ross Roses,
St Andrews Terrace,
(P.O. Box 23),
Willunga,
South Australia 5172.
Telephone: (085) 562555

and Roy and Heather Rumsey of:

Roy H. Rumsey Pty Ltd.,
Rose Specialist Growers,
1335 Old Northern Road,
Dural (P.O. Box 1),
New South Wales 2158.
Telephone: (02) 652 1137

Both of my contacts in Japan are men who have worked with roses over a long period of time:

Toru Onodera,
48 Kami-okubo,
Urawa-shi,
Saimtama,
Japan 338.
Telephone: 0488-53-9444

and Seizo Susuki,
Keisei Rose Research Dept.,
Keisei Rose Nurseries Inc.,
Yachiyo-city,
Chiba Pref. Japan.
Telephone: 0474-83-3147

Pat and Newt Wiley are my major contacts in the U.S.A. and their address is:

Roses of Yesterday and Today,
802 Browns Valley Road,
Watsonville,
California 95076.
Telephone: (408) 724-3537

In Canada, my fairly recent contact is:

Pickerings Nurseries,
670 Kingston Road,
Pickering,
Ontario.
Telephone: (416) 839 2111

Also a recent connection, my contact in South Africa is:

Ludwig's Roses (Pty) Ltd.,
P.O. Box 28165,
Sunnyside,
Pretoria 0132,
Republic of South Africa.
Telephone: 5-0168

In West Germany one of my contacts is Ingwer Jensen who is in Flensburg, right near the Danish border:

Ingwer J. Jensen,
Hermann Lons Weg 39,
Flensburg 2390.
Telephone: 0461 59586

My Danish contacts are Ellen and Hugo Lykke of Søby:

Ellen and Hugo Lykke,
Rosenplanteskole,
Hønebjergvej 31 Søby,
8543 Hornslet,
Danmark.
Telephone: 06 9746 29

In the United Kingdom my contacts are two men who serve the old rose well. They are:

Peter Beales Roses,
London Road,
Attleborough,
Norfolk NR 17 1AY.
Telephone: (0953) 454707

and David Austin Roses,
Bowling Green Lane,
Albrighton,
Wolverhampton WV7 3HB.
Telephone: (090722) 2142

And now that we have come to the end of this second volume, it is my dearest wish that you should have enjoyed the journey with me. I think it is important that at one time or another in your life, you stand still for a while and survey the past. If the medium you choose for this purpose is old roses, then I must be gratified. When visitors from near and far arrive to see our display garden, we are delighted that they, for a short time at least, have stepped aside from the hurly-burly of modern life to ponder the history in the garden, where time stands still and where all of us can be close to nature.

Euphrates

INDEX

Index

Index

Index